# Beguiling Voices

*Book Three of the Glass Bottles Series*

J Dark

Cover design © 2018 by Niki Lenhart
nikilen-designs.com

Published by Paper Angel Press
paperangelpress.com

ISBN 978-1-944412-43-2 (Trade Paperback)

10 9 8 7 6 5 4 3 2 1

FIRST EDITION

## Dedication

*This is dedicated to Paper Angel Press for believing in new authors,*
*to anyone who proofreads or edits,*
*and finally, this is for anyone who picks up this book.*
*Thank you from the bottom of my heart.*

## Acknowledgements

*Any book that comes to print has a lot of support behind it. The writer is just the tip of the iceberg. Paper Angel Press saw promise and offered the support of a great editor. The edits came back and were challenging.*

*A manuscript needs readers beyond editors, friends who will read and comment honestly on what they perceive. All the friends that read the manuscript and commented were invaluable with their support.*

*Support from family is equally important. My family encouraged me, and helped by giving space when needed, offering comments, jokes, and a wonderful sense of just being family.*

*Finally, the best support comes from readers, who take a chance on a book and read. Thank you all for everything.*

# 1

I POURED MYSELF A THIRD SHOT OF SCOTCH, raised it to my lips and poured the whole shot down. The familiar burn of the alcohol blurred the nightmare a little more. The man sitting in the guest chair on the other side of my desk wore a condescending smile and waited patiently for me to put the bottle back in the bottom drawer of the desk. He leaned forward; his immaculate silver-grey power suit, ivory shirt, and bright red silk necktie shifted smoothly as he rested his hands on knees, projecting an earnest concern. His gaze lowered to the bottle, and then moved to the empty shot glass still in my hand.

Why am I drinking in front of a client you might ask? Simple. He showed up early while my secretary was away from the office getting breakfast. If I hadn't been so hung over and sleep-deprived, I might have questioned the timing of his appearance.

Every time I closed my eyes to sleep, I'd see the two detectives, Kent Nix and Kevin Love, dangling from silver shackles — their vivisected bodies twitching, their organs pulsing wetly as their eyes locked on mine, begging me to end their pain.

This recurring dream had gotten so bad that drinking to dull my mind had become the only way I could get a bit of peace. That's what being possessed by a dead dragon will do to you. I don't recommend it.

Anyways, I'd planned on getting up early and putting the place in order. Instead, Sinera had cleaned it up while I was sleeping. My office still looked dingy, but at least now it was a clean sort of dingy. My office had a fresh coat of light ivory paint, scrubbed floors, and all the authentic accouterments that gave it its authentic 1930's *noir* ambiance: candlestick telephone and manual typewriter on my big wooden desk, old five-drawer file cabinets behind and to either side of said desk. My Murphy bed was in the far corner, with windows on both sides. The desk I used was near the middle of the floor, with two wooden chairs for clients to sit in, like the one currently here. If you've seen *The Maltese Falcon,* or read any Mickey Spillane or Dashiell Hammett, you have a good idea what my office looked like.

I was proud of my latest acquisition: a real 1930's overhead fan. It'd taken a couple months to track down, and cost me a hefty chunk of money. It was worth it. It even has a light.

Since the place was clean, I'd moved on to the next job — avoiding a monster headache. A few shots of scotch should have helped with that.

I'd just gotten the second one down when the client showed up … early. I did mind him being early, but it wasn't polite to insult a paying customer in the first thirty seconds they walk through the door. That reflects badly on the person and the business. The thing was: I wanted that third shot to settle my nerves, before getting down to business.

To buy myself a little more time, I gathered up the files I'd been annotating, and arranged them in their folders. I walked them out to Sinera's desk in the outer office for her to put away. We'd had a busy time of it.

Over the last two months, I'd worked two divorce cases that needed a little "nudging" to get the proceedings legally started. In the first, the woman had married her former husband to avail herself of his considerable trust fund. She'd carried on behind his back with her girlfriends during the whole marriage. All that needed was me luring the wife into a liaison … which turned out to be rather easy. She was into women.

The second divorce was a little messier, and included a "dognapping". The husband had declared he'd been cheated of what he'd asked for, and that "his" dog became "hers" out of spite. So one night the dog disappears from its kennel. Subsequent questioning of the husband and searches of his residence revealed he didn't have the dog. I dropped it off with him three weeks after the investigation, and man and dog are happily together.

I got back to my desk and sat down. I automatically reached for the shot glass and scotch, then looked up into my potential client's eyes. Under his gaze, my ears started to burn with both alcohol and shame. I picked up the cap and screwed it back on, sealing the bottle, wishing I could do the same thing to my dreams.

I placed the bottle back in the bottom desk drawer just as my new receptionist, Sinera, walked into the inner office with a heavenly-smelling cup of coffee and a box containing three sausages rolled up in pancakes — "pigs in blankets" for you non-Canadians.

Sinera is an Elf — which really was a shock to those that knew me. When she'd showed up at my door asking about a secretary's job, I had to stifle my automatic flinch reflex. Yeah,

I'm still a bit jumpy about being close to what nearly killed me, but Sinera has been very understanding about my recently acquired distrust of Elves.

She looked a lot like the late and very unlamented Elf Lord Cobb: tall — nearly as tall as my sister — and gracefully slender. She had deep wood-brown hair, the pointed ears you would expect when I said "elf", with intense blue eyes in a face sculpted by a master. It took me a moment to realize that I was both afraid of her Elven features, and jealous of her looks. In a fit of masochism, or of brilliance — or maybe both — I decided to swallow my knee-jerk reactions and gave her the job. It'd worked out pretty well.

After Sinera dropped off my breakfast, she walked back out, closing the inner door behind her silently. I picked the brown bag up and set it in the center drawer. Food could wait until after I'd finished with my potential new client. The distractions put away, I returned my attention to the situation at hand.

Looking at his eyes, I didn't see a caring soul in them. In fact, his gaze seemed calculating, reminding me of a televangelist or a slick, high-pressure salesman. His voice, a buttery-smooth melodic baritone that sounded almost too large for my cozy 1930's *noir* gumshoe office, seemed to fill the entire room.

"Ms. Fatelli," he began. "I'm David Cameron. I understand you're the one to come to in Halifax, Ms. Fatelli, when there is a delicate and unusual problem needing to be solved."

I expected that kind of inquiry, but at the same time, it was like a slime that clung to my hands and stank like rotted fish. I figured I could live with it. I'd done so many times before. Plus, this was relief: something to focus on rather than hide in my office, alone with my nightmares, and the Scotch — which was becoming a regular nightly habit. The Scotch started kicking in and my discomfort with this slick-feeling gentleman lessened.

"I will get right to the point. I'm worried about my niece. I believe she is being abused by her parents. I am asking you to get her out of that environment and deliver her to my residence, where I can keep her safe from my cousin's husband. I expect you're going to ask why I haven't visited the police about this situation. Believe me, I've tried. The signs are all there, but nothing to date has been proven. In fact, the police have said that, without any concrete evidence, there is no case."

I nodded, half listening, half relaxing into the warm alcoholic glow the scotch was giving me. That's why I get the business I do. The police have criteria that have to be met before they can legally intervene. I don't need a reason, other than someone is willing to pay me to do a job the police can't — or oftentimes won't — act upon.

I work in the grey area of the laws. I understood the unspoken words: he was asking me to kidnap his niece. I'd done it before, and for what I consider to be all the right reasons. That didn't make it any less illegal, despite it being the 'right thing' to have done. Kidnapping, like what I did to the General's family to hide them from the men he was set to expose, is still kidnapping.

There's nothing gray at all in the law about it. We got away with it because we weren't caught, and because it really was, in a sense, body-guarding them. This, however, is further into the 'bad' side of kidnapping. If I accepted the job, I'd be taking the girl away from her family, and handing her over to someone that claimed to be a concerned family member.

This is where 'due diligence' comes in. When someone tells you a story: confirm the details. Let me repeat that: confirm the details. In this line of work, there are a lot of people that would happily spin you a tale, then try to leave you holding the bag when the story breaks down.

And that's where alcohol is not your friend. It dulls your mind and deadens your instincts — the part of you that unerringly reads another person's intentions behind the social mask they wear. We, as humans, are so used to second-guessing ourselves, we don't pay attention to them anymore. I'm guilty of it too. It's easier to ignore what's uncomfortable than confront it. Cameron's voice was so soothing, and the alcohol's warm glow relaxed me so much, that I didn't pay attention to my own instincts. Instead, I focused on his story, and started asking questions.

"What signs of abuse are there? If the police don't have evidence, it sounds more like verbal and mental abuse."

He unclasped his hands, placing them on his knees. "When I see her, Ginny is always looking down, always jumping at any noise. She was taken out of the house once, after she tried to kill herself. The other signs are there too: a series of unsubstantiated illnesses, and she attempted to run away at least once. It's all in the police records. Please go verify what I'm saying before you accept this request. I want to be totally above board with you."

Having someone tell me they want to be above board always gets my hackles up. Usually they're the ones with the biggest things to hide. This time, I just couldn't summon the cynical suspicion that invariably came to me when I heard that statement.

I looked over at my door for a moment before shifting my gaze to Mr. Cameron.

"I'll do that," I told him. "Have Sinera make an appointment for next week: same day, same time." I waited until he started to stand. "Oh, by the way, Mr. Cameron, I'm going to need the name of the police precinct that has these reports, and Ginny's full name."

Mr. Cameron nodded. "The precinct is the Twenty-First, North Halifax. They'll have the records I spoke of. Her name is Genevieve Constance Cameron." He smiled, his teeth gleaming in the morning sunlight like mirrors. "Thank you, Ms. Fatelli. I hope you do take this job. It would mean so much to me to free her from that environment."

He sounded like a televangelist praying on his knees in front of the camera. Again, his demeanor was earnest, but the way he spoke, and the words he chose, should have set off the warning bells that something wasn't right.

Unfortunately, the scotch talked louder than my good sense.

# 2

O VER THE YEARS, one can run into all sorts of people. That's true in real life — and even more so in my line of work. Shady types abound because that gray area is where they have the best success at surviving and "making a living". In my case again, I'd gotten a lot of contacts with other, more legitimate, private investigators. Hiring them would put one level of removal between me and the police if I took the job.

Dean Youngwood is a full-blooded Cree — and a genuine hero. He'd taken a job a few years back when a woman's daughter had disappeared. The trail led to a sex slavery ring. Dean went in, spirited all the girls out, called the RCMP, and corralled the entire crew. The slavers, and a few high-ranking mob bosses, got indicted.

During the run-up to the trial, a number of potential witnesses in the mob died suddenly: three of natural causes, one was shot dead in a robbery attempt gone bad, and two burned alive in bed when they fell asleep smoking. You get the picture.

The "hero" part is why I went to Dean. This is the kind of thing he's had experience with, and, if the allegations Mr. Cameron had discussed with me were legitimate, he'd be good backup. I mean, the man's a freaking ghost. He's expensive, too. One of the top P.I. guys in all of New Scotland. We'd bumped heads on a few cases and, while we weren't friends, we were professional colleagues.

Dean's place is easy to find. Just go north on the Highway of Heroes to Burnside Drive, then turn east on Frazee. His office is in the building on the corner: main floor, east corner.

Dean himself is kind of non-descript. He stands about one-point-seven meters tall. He has a square face, with jet black hair cut in an unruly mop, and dark brown eyes. He's a little on the heavy side, but that serves him well, as few people ever give him a second glance. He served a hitch in the RCAF as a mechanic, then decided to leave. He got his private detective license, then stumbled into the aforementioned smuggling ring as his third case. Talk about jumping in at the deep end.

It did get him a lot of notoriety, which helped him get established. He cracked a few other cases, and his reputation was set. He helped anyone that he could, often working for free. His wife, Sveta, is Ukranian, and his secretary/financial wizard. Her family had moved to Halifax just before the Change. They'd survived, and Sveta was born here about ten years before Fawn and I. She'd grown up in Halifax, going through college, graduating with a finance degree, and had gone into business. You'd think a tall gorgeous woman like that was one of the girls he'd rescued, but you'd be wrong. They met through a dating service and hit it off. Sometimes the greatest treasures are found in the simplest places.

I parked outside the rock and corrugated metal building that housed Dean's office and walked inside to see him.

As I pushed the glass door open, Sveta glanced up from her work to give me a slight smile. She nodded at the wooden chairs surrounding a coffee table covered with magazines and old comic books. The rug was light tan, which matched the wooden chairs. The table was a modern glass and metal monstrosity set amongst all the natural furniture.

The walls were painted a shade darker than ivory, which gave the feeling of being out in the open. Mounted on each wall were sets of antlers: moose, elk, caribou, and deer. To the left of the door, on the black counter top, sat a twenty-cup coffee pot.

I sat down and pawed through the magazines, looking for something that wasn't a year old, then gave up and just grabbed one of the comic books. The over-the-top drama and bold colors made the comic fun to read, and I was thoroughly engrossed in it when Dean's office door creaked open.

He held the door open as an older man, dressed in a black-and-red wool shirt and thick flannel pants, stepped past him, then turned to shake his hand. Tears made the man's eyes shimmer in the lighting as Dean clasped his hand.

"Thank you, Mr. Youngwood. I appreciate you finding my daughter. Now, we can lay her to rest."

"I am sorry I couldn't bring her home, Josiah. Truly I am."

The old man released Dean's hand, then wiped his sleeve across his eyes. "The police said all there is to say. Thank you again Mr. Youngwood." He turned and shuffled to the door as Dean walked over to my spot by the coffee table.

"Fern Fatelli, this is the last place I'd expect to see you." He glanced at the cover of the comic, showing a red-and-blue hero taking on a grey behemoth with a horn on the center of its head. "Oh, good choice, that one has some good writing and art."

I smiled as I put the comic back on the table. "This is the last place I'd expect to see me too. But there's a case that you could help me with, if that doesn't cause any troubles with your regular work." I pulled out a folded sheet of paper. "This is a case of parental abuse, and I've got to cover another job. Could I ask you to drop by the Twenty-First precinct and pick up a file on Ginny Cameron? She's the minor in the middle of all this. I know it's asking a lot for legwork I could do, but I think you're a better choice to go pick the file up."

His front door opened, and a young woman entered. Before she could flag Dean down, he placed a hand on my arm.

"Let's talk in my office, Ms. Fatelli. I can get the whole story there."

He looked over to his wife, who observed the young woman with a disapproval that reminded me of a pissed-off cat getting ready to lay into a dog.

Dean ushered me into his office. Unlike mine, his had a clean and organized look. A pinewood desk sat near the window across from the door. The pale blue walls reminded me of the sky. A thick, deep brown rug covered the floor, making the large office feel smaller, and warmer. Two pine chairs sat in front of the desk. To the right was a sofa and a set of file cabinets. To the left was a floor-to-ceiling bookcase that doubled as a huge curio cabinet.

Dean walked over to the nearest chair, and pulled it out slightly for me. I gave him a warm smile as he walked behind his desk and sat down. He leaned forward, placing his elbows on the desk, and resting his chin on his hands.

"Now, Ms. Fatelli. How about you tell me why you came all this way just to ask if I'd do you a favor and pick up papers you easily could, especially with your connections to Halifax RCMP?"

I outlined the situation, and Dean, bless him, picked up on the trouble right away.

"You go get the file, and your sister comes after you *if* this Mr. Cameron is on the level."

"Yep, that sums it up nicely. If I find out what Cameron said is true, then I pull the girl out of that place and move the child to relatives. Otherwise, she continues to be abused."

Dean frowned as he thought through all we had talked about. Finally, he placed his hands on his desk, and looked at me.

"In this case, I can see why you'd ask me. I have the reputation that opens doors. I get the report, hand it to you, and you've got one level of removal from the case. Fawn doesn't come visit you; she comes and visits me."

I grimaced.

"Yeah, there is that. But it's easy to avoid. Since I'm doing the job, I'll call you ahead of time before I grab the girl. That way you'll have an unassailable alibi by being in front of a lot of people when it happens. Everyone knows you're a solo act."

Dean nodded, reluctantly. "All right, I'll do it. But you'll owe me one, Fatelli."

"Deal." We shook hands. "I'm going to check Cameron out while you get Ginny Cameron's files."

He nodded. "Good hunting, Fatelli."

"See you around, Youngwood."

I started to rise when two feminine voices started into a shouting match in the outer office. Youngwood grimaced, and motioned me to sit back down.

"Stay here. It'll be safer for your eardrums"

The voices rose in intensity until the two were screeching at each other. Dean sighed and looked up at the ceiling.

"You want to know why, don't you?"

When I nodded, Dean returned the nod absent-mindedly.

"She's one of the girls from the sex-trafficking bust. She's got a crazy idea that we're supposed to be together forever. Now she comes by about three or four times a month to talk me into marrying her. Other than the fact I don't like the pressure she puts on me, she's just not a person I want to know."

He shrugged as the angry voices reached a crescendo, then abruptly stopped. A slamming door indicated the woman's departure.

Dean looked over at me. "Save me from damsels in distress."

I think he meant it partly as a joke, but … I could empathize. Stalkers are a natural result of notoriety. Some think you should be shot because you got attention when they didn't, while others want to possess you because they want to be noticed — and get all the benefits of a famous partner. Dean had his own problems with her. Very polite to everyone, I just couldn't see him shouting at anyone. He wasn't the yelling type.

I thought more about his problem. I'd had to discourage a few stalkers in the day. Well, usually Zhirk did — who was a wonderful deterrent. Me asking them to stop didn't have the same gravitas as when a nearly three-meter-tall Troll did. Most stopped immediately after a brief talk with my ex-partner. The one that didn't was obsessed enough to pull a pistol and shoot him. For all I know, he may still be in traction.

"Hey, Dean? As a free-of-charge favor, since you're doing me one, how about I go talk to your stalker, and convince her to lay off?"

Dean looked at me like I'd sprouted a second head. "Fatelli, no offense meant, but you are the kind of woman that attracts people, not the kind to scare them off."

I shrugged and smiled. "I've a few favors owed. How about me and my marker go talk to her?"

Dean shrugged. "If you can peacefully resolve this mess, I'd certainly be grateful."

I nodded, then stood up. "I will see what I can do about it."

Dean gave me a tired smile and waved me towards the door. "Don't talk to Sveta. She's always like a mother grizzly after a bout with Helen."

"Good to know. Thank you again, Dean."

He sat down and opened a drawer as I turned to leave. The sound of chalk on a surface came to me as I closed the door. The scowling Sveta glared at me as I offered her the barest of waves and hurried to the door.

Once outside, I crawled into my "cleaned up" PT Cruiser. The back seats had been pulled a long time ago, so it was a two-seater with a lot of rear space. The new flat grey paint job made it look even older. It also made it look more ratty — which was perfect for my job.

My next order of business was to check out Mr. Cameron.

# 3

THERE USED TO BE ANY NUMBER OF ORGANIZATIONS that you could call to haul background information about nearly anything together from the internet: things like your shoe size, favorite toothpaste — everything was tracked.

With all the craziness that happened when magick came back, those places fell apart, and just don't exist anymore. The internet still exists, but it's not nearly as comprehensive as it used to be. A lot of old server sites went away, so information is prioritized to be on the 'net. The good side: a lot less advertising. The bad side: nearly all personal information is once again kept in hardcopy at various locations.

The kind of personal stuff I wanted was on the local government sites, but they logged you in and kept track of who looked at what. There's hardcopy though, and all one has to do is drive to City Hall, walk down to the basement, and make a request to the librarian to look at the records. This still involves signing in and out, but here I can fake a name, with a fake ID, and get into the files. Yes, this is illegal, but, to keep my sister out of this, it was smarter.

The librarian was an Orc. For those of you that haven't met an Orc before, Orcs were one of the first of the Changed to appear. They were, on average, two meters tall and one hundred-fifty kilograms. Their bodies were like the great apes: arms half again as long as their legs. They usually walk upright on those short, powerful legs, but when they need to move fast, they drop to all fours and can match speeds with a horse for a short sprint. Their faces are reminiscent of a chimpanzee's. They have two vertical slits for a nose, and wide lips covering triangular teeth like a shark's. Their eyes are slit like those of a cat, and are usually yellow, but I've seen some with tan-colored eyes. An Orc's ears are short triangles on the sides of their head, about the size and shape of a cat's ear, and stand horizontally out from the sides of their head. The color of their skin ranges from tan to yellow-green, with all of the shades in between.

Orc males have a narrow strip of dark hair on their heads. Their females are bald, and are generally stockier than the males. They're obligate carnivores — meaning they can't digest plant matter — and can go through an entire cow in a week. Pretty intimidating.

This is where appearances deceive. They're intelligent, articulate, and very social. Orcs know what their appearance does to the other races, and go to great lengths to tone down the scary. They are, as a race, very "human" in their actions. The only thing they can't do is cast magick.

Every race has a quirk like that: trolls are dyslexic, fairies have abysmally short attention spans. Orcs are also very slow to reproduce. They live as long as humans typically do, but are considered fortunate to have more than two children in their lifetime. They reproduce by laying a soft, leathery egg. This has kept their numbers down, so you don't see them often.

This one sat behind the checkout desk, wearing a full police uniform. She looked up from whatever she had been reading and regarded me with slitted yellow eyes.

"What can I do for you, dear?" Her voice possessed a very feminine tenor.

She stood up, giving me her undivided attention. I could see her name on her badge: *Jaeger*.

She noticed my gaze and chuckled. "Supposedly it's said with the 'J' sounding like 'Y', being German. But I like how the 'J' sounds. So it's 'Jay-ger'.

"That's something I didn't know before. So Ms. Jaeger, can I sign out the public records on a Mr. David Cameron?"

The Orc smiled. "Just sign here, then I'll get however many Camerons there are, and you can look for your David fellow in the side room."

I signed in as "I. Strom" on the ledger. She nodded at a door with a large pane of frosted glass in the upper half. The glass was dark.

When Ms. Jaeger went back to hunt up Camerons, I went over to the room, opened the door and turned the light on. It contained one large metal table and two brushed aluminum chairs. LED lights in each ceiling tile shed their glow throughout the room. I took my "Gone Fishin'" ball cap off, set it on the table, and draped my red-and-black checked coat on the chair. Then I walked back out to the checkout desk to wait for Ms. Jaeger to return.

Ms. Jaeger brought a full box back to the counter, and carefully set it down.

"There are twelve David Camerons in Halifax. So please look through them, and return them intact, Ms. Strom."

I returned her smile. "Can do, Officer Jaeger."

I took the box of files into the room and left the door open so Ms. Jaeger could see I wasn't doing anything unsavory to her precious files.

Going through the files took a few hours. There were tax reports, some minor violations, but nothing that gave me the feeling I was being lied to. There were no old arrests, no suspicions of anything. All twelve David's did their work, paid the government what they owed it and, without any other evidence, they were clean as a proverbial whistle.

Their jobs ranged from building maintenance, restaurant manager, author, pastor, programmer, machinist, and business executive. I wasn't certain which was my client since there were no pictures. That didn't mean my guy was totally without flaw; he might be anything — it's just nothing that the RCMP or other governmental agencies cared about. So, unless I did my own investigation into Mr. David Cameron's background, I had to conclude that, despite my own gut-feeling, he wasn't a known threat to anyone. I put each file back together and put them back in the box before taking it back out to Officer Jaeger.

"Find anything interesting, Ms. Strom?" Her tenor had a note of amusement in it.

"Nothing that would help me. Thank you, officer."

She nodded then picked up the box with both hands. "I'll put this back and you can sign out. Have a nice day, Ms. Strom."

So the question became: How deep do I want to investigate Cameron?

My gut kept telling me that something was off, but a gut feeling isn't something that you can point to and say, "This is my evidence". It won't stand up in a Court of Law, no matter how accurate it is. And, to be truthful, Zhirk hit me the same way when I first met him. He'd set off every alarm I had and, yet, he was actually a good guy. I missed him. That, more than anything else, convinced me to give Cameron the benefit of the doubt and trust his word.

I find it constantly amazing at how often these "gut feelings" prove out, and how often people, like me, find excuses to ignore them.

# 4

G ETTING BACK TO MY OFFICE, Sinera reminded me that electric and rent were due in two weeks. I had the money. What I do pays very well, but I'm not so complacent that I didn't work.

Two things kept me going. One: however much I had in the bank, it's finite. If you don't make money, you'll be up a creek if you don't at least break even between making and spending.

And two: being alone with nothing to do let my thoughts wander, and since the events on Prince Edward Island, they kept wandering back to everything that happened there. I keep having nightmares.

After being given the cheerful "bills are due" from Sinera, I went back to my office, sat down at my desk, then went through what I'd found so far. With a load of nothing, another way to attack the problem is from the endpoint backwards. So the next step was to wait for Ginny's records to get here from Dean.

I didn't have all that long to wait. Dean, being the conscientious guy he is, had gone down to the precinct right after I left, and requested copies of Ginny's files, citing a possible link to something similar he'd run across. His earnest, non-descript face got him legal copies, and then he did what I had done: gone down to the records department at City Hall, and pulled everything they had on Ginny.

Dean sent me the information by courier, and included a note saying that he'd work *pro bono* if what I had been told was true. He thought it might be, from the police reports. There was a definite hint of troubles at home: she'd run away twice, tried to kill herself once, and acted out at school. Cameron had been telling the truth about that too. I really wished he'd been scamming me. This looked ugly.

After reviewing the kid's incidents, I turned my attention to the residence. Yeah, I'd decided to go forward, and would call Cameron later. Despite my misgivings about David Cameron, the kid was definitely in an abusive home. Getting her out would be my job. Hey, it's hardball. But kidnapping for a good cause is still kidnapping. Don't get me wrong; I haven't changed my morals. I may set people up for a divorce now and again, but I've never turned down anyone in need, and this girl, Ginny Cameron, looked desperately in need when I read between the lines.

Ginny was the only child of Hubert Cameron, the current CEO and president of CCoal, Canada Coal.

What? You think after all that magick our infrastructure was totally untouched? Coal is our best natural power source, along with oil shale. Things may be getting better with solar power, but the magick incident over here clobbered the fast scientific advances. So we rely mostly on coal and oil for heating and energy for factories. Not the cleanest, not the best, but cheap and, most importantly, abundant. Though to be fair, abundant doesn't always equate to safe.

What all that meant was that the family was seriously rich, and likely had serious security. The address was easy enough to check out. The residence in question was located in White Field, which is across the Bedford channel from Halifax, and southeast. The area is a haven for the ultra-rich, with huge grounds surrounding large palatial homes. Places like that tend to have a lot of protection. I began getting a sinking feeling in my stomach. People that affluent tend to hire security, part to protect themselves, but more to protect their possessions.

I drove the twenty minutes over to the Cameron residence to check the security out. It was as bad as my imagination had conjured. Broken bottles were cemented to the top of the three-meter wall. Two teams of men with a dog walked the ground at all hours of the day and night. The wall surrounded the back and sides of the mansion, with a two-meter tall tasteful iron fence across the front. A single gate at the driveway was controlled by someone in the house. Getting in — and then back out — with Ginny would be a real challenge. This would mean finding one or, ideally, two people trustworthy enough to include on this job. One just could not pull it off. Too many variables and too many guards if I got unlucky or careless. The other option was like we had done with Megan Maystack: we kidnapped her and her mother, Anne, to hide them from assassins.

In that job, we studied both women for habits or routines, and based our actions on what we had found out. I was hoping we could do the same with Ginny.

Ginny attended Haven School, a preparatory school for young girls. The school was only for humans. One of those little havens where rich, powerful, and xenophobic parents send their children to keep them away from the disgusting reality of the world.

It was time to go do a little legwork. I don't like public locations for a situation like this, but it was likely a lot better than trying to storm the mansion with all the security there. But I wouldn't know until I checked it out.

After driving over and discreetly watching the school from the park across the street, I had an idea of the school's layout, the girls' clothing, and rough times of the classes. The school was surrounded on all sides by a two-meter hurricane fence, presumably to stop anyone from snatching a girl right off the grounds. A forest lay just beyond the fence at the back of the school, with one gate on the north side for maintenance to bring in equipment when needed.

Two RCMP officers stood at the front gate when children were dropped off and when the school let out. Crap. That made things complicated. Police would surely call for backup with a kidnapping or any suspicious activity.

The students had a particular uniform of a navy blue skirt, white blouse, and white socks with black shoes. They were allowed to style their hair and accessorize it with barrettes, but no jewelry, no hair coloring and, wonder of wonders, I saw no cell phones. That actually was a break. Without fast communication, escaping after grabbing Ginny would be easier with a good head start. Students stayed in the school or on the grounds all day. At the end of the day, the girls were picked up individually at the front of the school.

Fortunately, I was not under a time limit. I could plan and prepare. Thankfully for this situation, I'm short, so no one notices me for my size. It's the curves and such that get me attention. I did look young enough to pass for high school, with some makeup to disguise my age.

The first part was simple enough: get myself looking like a student. Honestly, though, the thought of dressing up as a student reminded me of some of those fetish places where the women dressed up as school girls for the clientele. *Ugh.*

The second was getting myself enrolled late, which might be problematic. Then inspiration hit me. I could get an influential sponsor! One with impeccable credentials would make it easy to get myself registered.

Usually, going to a former client isn't my style at all. Most are only too happy to see the last of me. But, considering our history, I might convince the former Mrs. Thensome to help me out. I'd helped her with a divorce case — which had turned into a waking nightmare for me and a lot of people. It got Zhirk, my best friend, killed. I rubbed the stump of my little finger.

Double crap. I'd have to concoct a story about why it was missing.

My second idea came then. I could flaunt the wound and, if Mrs. Thensome agreed, concoct a story about parental abuse and that would give me a chance to get closer to Ginny if I could get into the school. Shared experience and all. The first job now would be to talk to Mrs. Thensome. Then it would be time to go find help. The best place for that kind of muscle and moxie would be The Candle Club. First things first, though. Talk to Mrs. Thensome, and see if I could get her to sponsor me.

# 5

G OING TO SEE MRS. THENSOME and asking for help was very different than the first time had been. When I came here before with Zhirk, we were trying to get more background on Hervald Thensome. He'd tried attacking us twice, and I wanted to find a way to catch him and get him out of my hair. She'd given us reports that other private investigators had compiled on her ex-now-deceased-husband.

The place was like it had been the first time: a tall metal fence surrounding the house, the open gate, the long driveway to a circular rotunda with a fountain in the center, and the cobbled stone walk with the two cement sitting lions where *Wurmlings* had previously resided. I resisted using the Sight to see if those vicious little outsiders were there. Honestly, I didn't want to know.

Knocking on the large double doors brought a familiar face. Mr. Rich — all two meters, stubby five o'clock shadow, cinder block features, and black butler's suit of him — answered the door. I thought I saw an eyebrow twitch in mild surprise at seeing me again.

"I must remind you, Ms. Fatelli, that we allow no solicitations here." Mr. Rich's voice was a hollow baritone, totally devoid of emotion.

I swallowed dryly. Now was the time to pull it together and see if this crazy idea I concocted would actually work.

"I understand. However, I'm here on a matter that I hope Mrs. Thensome would listen to, if she has the inclination." See? I can be diplomatic.

Mr. Rich thought for a long moment, then nodded his craggy head.

"I will inform Mrs. Thensome of your request. Please wait here." He looked behind him, and then jerked his head back in my direction.

Mr. Rich moved back to allow a magickan to step out on the landing with me. Hunched over, she — I knew somehow that the figure was female — tottered onto the landing with a slow, jerky grace that reminded me of those old shows about cursed Egyptian mummies coming to life to exact revenge on those that disturbed their rest.

Her deep royal-blue hooded robe shimmered in the daylight. She straightened up from her hunch, putting her at eye level with me. Two large, pupil-less blue eyes peered back. A *Hamref.* They're one of the smaller races that came back, and are one of the many that can cast spells.

They're humanoid, but their skins are three times as thick, tough enough to stop standard pistol rounds. Their nostrils spread way out on their elongated face, a slit being found a finger's width under each double-sized eye. Like Orcs, they are obligate carnivores. The key difference between the two races is that where Orcs are encountered singly, Hamref are found in packs. Dayning was replete with small Hamref communities dotted throughout it.

"Good day, Ms. Fatelli." Her voice was soft, like water rippling over rocks.

I gazed at her while my brain worked on the most suitable reply, and then gave up.

"Hello, Miss …?" I queried her.

"Jaco. And it is Mrs., as you would say it." The Hamref smiled and pushed her hood back. "You're Larry Potter's sister-in-law?"

I nodded.

"Splendid. I've met him a few times at his shop. He's a good friend to us."

Curiosity made me ask, "How do you know him?"

Mrs. Jaco started to reply, but was interrupted by Mr. Rich.

He gazed emotionlessly at the two of us for a second or two, then intoned, "Mrs. Thensome will see you, Ms. Fatelli."

He stepped onto the porch and gestured me through the door. The Hamref dutifully fell in behind me as Mr. Rich led the way to Mrs. Thensome's den.

She sat at her desk, with two laptops open. Mrs. Thensome wore a blue sweater over a coral-colored shirt as she industriously typed away on the keyboard. As we approached, she glanced up at Mr. Rich.

"Thank you, Mr. Rich. Ms. Fatelli, please take a seat. Mr. Rich and Mrs. Jaco will be right outside the door if you require anything."

I nodded politely, then sat down as both Mr. Rich and Mrs. Jaco left the room and closed the door. It was a sign of respect that she didn't keep either one in the room with me, and I appreciated the gesture.

Mrs. Thensome returned to gazing at her computers as she asked, "This is a very unusual visit. I would guess that there is something new in Hervald's case?"

I shook my head. "No, Mrs. Thensome. I came here to see if I could get your assistance for a case."

As her eyebrows went up in surprise, I launched into the presentation.

"First off, I have to ask you to keep everything I say in the strictest confidence. If you agree, I'll explain."

She hesitated, thinking this over. She knew what my job was; she'd hired me after all. So, to her thinking, this might be something similar. The thing is, according to law, if you help someone, either knowingly or unknowingly, commit a crime, you're as guilty as they are. In Mrs. Thensome's case, and with a lot of wealthy and/or influential people, money can buy you a break, if you know who to bribe. Ethical? Oh, heck no. Practical? Definitely.

She glanced over to me and nodded, saying, "This kind of offer doesn't come my way very often. I will counter offer. You tell me what it is you're planning to do, in general terms, and I'll make my decision to get involved based on that information."

I didn't like it, but it was fair.

"In general terms, then. I'm going to remove a minor from an abusive household and move her to other family members so she can be properly cared for."

Mrs. Thensome, to my surprise, nodded right away, her eyes gleaming, like a predator on the hunt. "I accept. What do you require?"

"Do you know about Haven School?" She nodded.

"Yes, I know it. I went there for all my high school years. Why?"

Not to bore you with recounting all that I've described earlier, I laid out the plan to her.

She listened attentively, then nodded. "So my involvement would be registering you as my ... niece, is it?"

When I nodded, she continued.

"You were removed from an abusive home, placed in my care, whereupon I registered you in Haven."

She leaned back in her chair, tapping her cheek with a manicured finger.

"I can see any number of ways this could end up in court for kidnapping. I happen to know Hubert and Alice — and detest them completely." She looked at me. "I expect that this will go public, along with the reasons?"

I nodded, and Mrs. Thensome smiled like a fox with a master key to the hen house.

"Good. I want it public. I want it as luridly public as can be managed, Ms. Fatelli."

I think my smile mirrored Mrs. Thensome's.

"Oh, I plan to. I hate it when children are abused."

Mrs. Thensome nodded, and began typing rapidly on her left-hand laptop.

"I'll send a note today to Mrs. Gross, the headmistress. I will handle the introduction, and you can pass me the pertinent information to properly enroll you." She leaned back and regarded me with an actual mischievous grin. "This is rather exciting to think about. I'm helping a crusading trapper steal a child out of dire circumstance." She sounded so happy, like a real crusader.

But my little internal cynic told me to ask her why. "Mrs. Thensome, if you'll pardon me for asking, why are you deciding to help me?"

"Why, leverage, of course. The Camerons are one of the pillars of the community. This will damage that pillar, and I can use this information it to my benefit."

Her eyes had that predatory gleam I'd seen earlier. I guess even altruism loses out to social politics.

I was still in a slight state of shock that she'd agreed so quickly and completely. It took me the whole walk back to my old PT Cruiser to snap out of my daze and get focused back on my job.

My next stop would be The Candle Club.

# 6

T HE CANDLE CLUB WAS A BAR. Not just a bar, but an authentic,
honest–to-deity, smugglers speakeasy from the early
twentieth century.

It consisted of two rooms separated by a revolving wall. The
front and public room was a restaurant with a bar for those
waiting for a table. The back was only two-thirds the size of the
front, but was a full bar with its own small stage for a band, and
some room for dancing. It's still kind of a speakeasy. The back is
where a lot of contacts are made on the wrong side of the law.
It's quiet, with a number of booths separated by paneled walls,
and a television for what passes for entertainment. All-in-all, it's
an interesting old piece of Halifax history.

It's also one of a couple dozen places where, with the right
connections, you can find the right person for the right under-

the-table, grey area, or just plain black jobs. The community is surprisingly close-knit. If you know someone, they'll know someone who knows about someone, and … You get the picture. No one talks about it, though. Talking gets you ostracized, and then anyone with a grudge and/or money can take you out without anyone in the community batting an eye or lifting a finger to help.

A friend of a friend, of a friend, in this murky underbelly, gave me the name of a friend who knew a friend that could help me out.

"Go to the Candle Club, get a table for two in the South corner, and wait."

I sat for a half-hour before someone approached me. A large, and vaguely familiar, someone. It took me a moment to place him. It's hard to forget an Orc that dresses in a black suit with a black shirt and a black tie, but I had managed it.

When Zhirk and I were hunting Baldy/Ahiah, we ran into him at a bar that catered specifically to non-humans. If I remembered his name correctly, he called himself 'JC'. When I last saw JC, he carried a guitar case that shifted in his grip, and something inside chittered maniacally, raising the hairs on the back of my neck. Whatever he kept in that guitar case, I never wanted to find out.

JC's green-yellow skin stood out tastefully in contrast to his all-black attire. His red eyes centered on me as he gave me a warm smile and began to sit down.

"Ms. Fatelli, I'm —" He has a wonderful baritone voice that had just a touch of the southern United States drawl to it. I didn't wait to give him a chance to introduce himself.

I smiled and said, "Hello, JC. Please, sit down and join me."

He blinked, then chuckled ruefully, setting his bulk in a special chair the staff hurriedly brought when he stopped at my table. This chair was identical to a standard one — just a half-size larger to handle the extra mass a Troll or an Orc carried.

JC leaned forward and placed his hands under his chin as he waited. I noticed a human waiter striding to our table. He stopped next to JC's chair.

"What can I get you to drink, sir and madam?"

"I'll have water, thank you," JC told him.

"I'll have some coffee, please."

The waiter made a few scribbles on his pad, then set the dinner menus in front of us.

"I've never been here before." I kept my voice low and not quite come-hither husky.

JC smiled as he picked up the menu and perused it. "I have, a few times. I have a fondness for the turkey. There aren't many places that will set you a whole bird."

He glanced over the menu.

I nodded. "I'm more of a fish person myself. That, and greens."

"Well then, I can say this place has a delightful Lake Trout. I've had that a few times."

I waved a hand and the waiter stepped over quickly, pad and pencil at the ready.

"I'll be covering the check tonight, lady's choice." I smiled at JC. "I'll have the pan-fried Lake Trout, and my guest will order for himself."

JC picked up on the little challenge, and smiled: *Challenge accepted.*

"I'll have two of the sixty-four-ounce Porterhouse, with bacon as a side dish." He gave the waiter an easy smile.

The waiter nodded and walked back to the kitchen to put in the order. Now that we had some time, we made small talk for a few minutes, feeling each other out. JC stopped the conversation when the waiter brought us our food.

"I do appreciate you covering the meal, Ms. Fatelli. I do offer my condolences to you. Zhirk was an honorable Troll, and good company in bad situations."

I rubbed the nub of my little finger under the table. "Yes, he was all that: a good friend, and a great comfort in difficult circumstance."

It was funny. Not funny *ha-ha*, but funny sad. Here I was, getting ready to talk about a kidnapping, and Zhirk being mentioned brought a lump to my throat that I couldn't swallow. I spent a moment or two waiting for the sadness to pass, then, carefully, laid it out for JC.

"There's a human child that's being abused by her parents. I'm looking at having a second pair of eyes and hands available for the work. Two things up front. One, we don't kill anyone. This is a kidnapping. While it's for a good reason, the RCMP will be all over us tenfold if someone dies. Two, I'll be glad to listen to your ideas. But as the employer, I have the final say on what we do, and when it happens."

JC regarded me, a bit of respect creeping into his voice. "Well now, I can see both of those points, and agree with them. I've done a few things in the past, and helping out a young girl from a situation of peril, why that might balance the books a little." He held out a muscular hand. "I'm in. Thank you, Ms. Fatelli."

We shook hands, sealing the deal.

"Thank you, JC. Where should I pick you up tomorrow?"

The waiter came by with the check and I put cash down on the plate, plus a generous tip for the waiter, who'd been very attentive to us.

JC thought for a moment. "I could start tonight, if that's not an imposition. The place I'm staying at is short on beds for folks."

I blinked in surprise, then thought about it. He was staying at a flophouse, which meant he was a little down on his luck. I knew a small motel near my office. I could put him up there for a few nights.

"All right. I'll drive you back to your place, and you can gather up your gear. I'll put you up at the Port Arms Motel. It's a half-block from my office."

JC nodded with excessive dignity.

"I do thank you, Ms. Fatelli. I don't have much but my guitar and a backpack. It should all fit in a trunk."

We got up and went out to gather up his belongings, and move him to his new place.

# 7

T HE NEXT MORNING, I got up early, cleaned, got a shower at
the local 'Y', then dressed in black slacks, white shirt, and
brown suspenders. My heeled boots went well with the ensemble.

JC was there promptly at nine, as I had asked. We spent the
next four hours going over all the information on Ginny, her
parents, the plan to enroll me in the school to learn more about
Ginny's habits and possibly befriend her. Initially, I saw JC as the
wheel man, and maybe muscle if things went pear-shaped. The
school was all human, from the staff to the students. No
non-human was ever on campus.

JC thought about things after I had wound down. He'd
brought his guitar along, an old Rickenbacker that he'd picked
up somewhere. It had seen a lot of wear and tear, its varnish
cracked and flaking, with a hole where the missing pick guard

should have been. When he ran his fingers across the strings, its rich mellow tone was perfect for his voice. He began strumming it as he considered my current plan.

"I think you have a hole in all this, Ms. Fatelli."

"No need for the formalities. Call me Fern, JC. We're working together."

JC nodded, then spoke in that wonderful whiskey-mellow voice of his.

"Well then, that seems fair enough, Fern. Now about that hole. What I'm seeing ..."

We went back and forth on the idea of snatching her in broad daylight. JC wanted to grab her a block or so away from the school. The idea was to follow her limousine and force it to stop, then take her out of the car. It was an improvement on my original plan to take her out the back of the school and cut through the fence. I originally threw it out, as I am not a great shot with a pistol, and the snubnose .357 Magnum I carry made aiming more luck than skill. It's a three-meter or less weapon. Anything else is too far to be accurate, unless you're some movie hero that can't miss. I'm not, and I do — miss, that is.

One bit of information we needed was the number of bodyguards in the car, and if there was any protection magick on it. The latter I could check out; the former would need some surveillance to determine. As we were talking a little about what we planned to do, Sinera knocked on the door, then opened it. She strode over to me and held out a large envelope.

"A Mr. Rich delivered this from Mrs. Thensome."

I took the proffered envelope. "Thanks, Sinera."

She nodded, then walked back to her desk, closing the office door behind her.

I turned the envelope over and undid the metal clasp. Removing the papers from it, I surveyed them.

I, Pyrrha Holdwell, would be enrolling mid-quarter at Haven. I think I owed Mrs. Thensome a favor for the help, but didn't mention it to her. One favor owed was one too many — especially with a shark like her.

I tossed JC the keys, grabbed my school backpack, then we went down to the PT Cruiser, and drove over to the school. Before JC showed up, I'd prepared by getting my makeup on, and put on the school girl uniform. I didn't button the top two buttons, allowing my breasts to be seen. I figured if I could get the instructor's eye, and get detention on the first day in school, I'd be that much closer to meeting Ginny.

Most of the girls accessorized as much as they could to stand out despite the rules. I took the same tack, and had four barrettes holding my fire-colored hair back to make a thick French braid. The braid did help me look younger, and the blue skirt brought out the green in my eyes. I could turn heads with this ensemble.

JC let me out at the front gate. The students noted the battered, dull-colored PT Cruiser drop me off. The Cruiser stood out like a sore thumb among the limousines and expensive cars. I'd have to rent a decent-looking vehicle to fit in. Fortunately, I could put that as a business expense to Mr. David Cameron. Hey, I'm not going to swallow a charge like that. I'm here to make money, not do charity cases.

My cover as Mrs. Thensome's niece should be decent. Mrs. Thensome had decided to go through her own contacts for the forgeries, and they must have been convincingly authentic, as no one said anything about any irregularities.

As I approached the gate, I got my 'game face' on. Pyrrha Holdwell, niece of Mary Thensome, was transferring in, and Fern Fatelli checked out.

At the front door, I was met by a chunky, bitter-looking old woman. Mrs. Gross' face matched her name. It was like a hatchet mounted on a thick neck that led to an even thicker body. Only it wasn't all fat. She was muscle and sinew, even at her age. Mrs. Gross was the principal of Haven, and she immediately read me the riot act.

"Ms. Holdwell, there will be no unbuttoned shirts, no chewing gum, no cell phones, no music-playing devices, and no electronics of any kind allowed on campus. Your first day is no excuse. Hand over all your items to Ms. Villers, my assistant, then you'll be allowed to go to your classroom, Ms. Holdwell." Her voice had a gruff, sharp quality that made her sound like a large dog.

I gritted my teeth, surprised at my own reaction. I never thought much of it before, but those electronic luxuries were what my life was connected to on a daily level. I could see why some of the girls might choose to act out at home after that little "Welcome to Haven" speech. Mrs. Gross made an impression … all bad. Now the question became what to do about it — and how to find Ginny Cameron.

Despite reading the reports the RCMP had on file at the Twenty-First Precinct, I wanted my own visual confirmation. Ginny deserved that much. If she'd been truly abused, then I would do my utmost to get her out of the school, and away from her parents, as fast as I could manage. If not, I'd call the client and return the fee, minus expenses.

The first class for me was History, and the great Magick Disaster of 2016. I kept quiet and sat in the back. The more I acted like a surly teen, the better my chances of Ginny buying in on the fake identity, and me being able to confirm her situation. Score one for attitude.

After History, came Social Studies, then Algebra, then lunch. Each room was an introduction, assigning a seat, then working on my angst. I guess I am a better actress than I thought. Most of the girls believed the act, or at least no one questioned it. All the while, I kept an eye open for Ginny.

I finally saw her after the last class of the day. She was in the school uniform, with bright neon-orange barrettes that clashed with her blonde hair, French braid, and school uniform. She didn't talk to any of the other students, walking purposefully, eyes staring straight ahead, towards the front doors. I wasn't sure how to approach her, but luck, fate, or magick — or any combination of the three — intervened in the form of the entitled clique come to read the rules to the new girl.

"Ooh look, she thinks she's all that," the leader said.

Said leader of the clique was tall, statuesque, with black hair and Asian features. Her hangers-on were a pair of identical twins. They were a full head taller than me, and a half-head shorter than the leader. They moved to stop me from heading towards the doors, or towards Ginny. Ginny saw what was happening and slowed, clearly wanting to avoid becoming another target for the bitch queens. I hate to admit it, but the girls' verbal attacks were getting to me. It was a replay of my years in high school. Maybe because of the magick, Fawn and I developed earlier than the other girls, were already dating boys … and breaking up with them.

The mean-girl cliques picked on me since, between the two of us, I was the smaller, and safer, target. Fawn got her share of teasing too, but she learned the facts before I did, and realized that getting aggressive was a sure way to get them to back off. She confronted the cliques head-on, and, being taller than the other girls by at least a head, her size drove the point home: *Mess with me, face the consequences.* She was as quick with her own sallies, as she was in field hockey. She beat them verbally in the hallways, and beat them physically on the field. She gave back what she got, with interest, and the girls quickly learned not to push. Fawn had her own clique that she reluctantly accepted. I wasn't in it.

Oh, we are sisters, but sisters fight — often a lot more viciously because they're sisters. While Fawn could protect herself, and her clique, I couldn't. That's what got me into martial arts for a while. I was doing well, until Fawn decided to join me and took to it like a duck to water. She blew past me in the belt tests, which killed my enthusiasm for it. But the time I was in martial arts gave me the confidence to stand up to the cliques. I got beaten and humiliated a lot, but not as bad as some. Being willing to fight back, and not let them beat you down, makes you a bigger target, but when things don't get any easier, the cliques tend to back off.

I backed up against the lockers. I could take them on, but that wouldn't look good at all. I wasn't here to become the alpha; I was here to kidnap/rescue Ginny. Ginny had stopped in the hall, and stepped back away from the confrontation. She, like most of the other girls, tried to remain unnoticed, and ignore the situation.

Getting picked on by the ruling clique was a sure path to perpetual misery for the school year.

The lead girl was tall and willowy. Her straight ash-blonde hair hung to her shoulders. She looked down at me like royalty looking down a peasant. Her lips curled in a gleeful sneer.

"Oh look, fake titties. She really must be hard up."

"Yeah, Kinsey, and so short. She's like … pocket-sized."

I mentally gritted my teeth as I kept up the deer in the headlights act. I glanced over at Ginny, who met my eyes, then flushed and looked down. My face was grabbed by Kinsey and turned to look her in the eyes.

"Don't look over there, skank. No one will help you. This is just going to be you and us."

One of the twins finally noticed my missing finger.

"Hey look, she's messed up. Her finger."

I cradled the hand against my chest and covered it with the other. Kinsey took that as a chance to show off, and grabbed my hand, pulling it taut. She made a show of examining the stump of the missing finger. I started to really get angry.

I caught myself and forced the anger back down. If I was helpless, Ginny wouldn't be as hard to approach. So, with difficulty, I stuck to the plan and didn't stick a fist in Kinsey's face. Kinsey finished the exam, and let go of my arm. The three girls walked off with a few last jeers directed at me. I looked back towards Ginny and saw Mrs. Gross lumbering my direction. That was why the girls quit so quickly.

"Day One, and you're already causing trouble, young lady. Come with me." Her voice and demeanor brooked no resistance.

I meekly nodded and followed her to the principal's office. Once inside, she closed the door.

The room was about three meters by three. A single window adorned the south wall. The walls were split horizontally at waist height. The upper half of the wall was all recessed bookcases, which went all the way round the room, broken only by the entrance and the window. The carpet was a sickly, yellow-brown color that looked like one huge nicotine stain. The walls and bookcases were a brilliant white that just made the carpet look more grungy.

Only about a quarter of the book cases held books. The majority were empty, excepting unread and unwrapped magazines, letters, and what looked like old sandwich wrappers. Mrs. Gross lived up to her name. Ugh.

"I am certain you know why you're here, young lady."

Mrs. Gross's voice had gotten sounding even more dog-surly. I suppressed a giggle at a mental image of a bloodhound dressed up like her.

"Is there something funny, Ms. Cameron?" she scowled at me.

I took the accusation and lowered my head. It didn't take much to act sullen.

High school is the last bit of childhood before the pressure of adult life. Puberty is in full swing, and the emotions run rampant and deep. I don't think anyone forgets high school. Everyone has something great and terrible that they remember. Mine was the bullying for being short and pretty. Fawn's was being so athletic that she was better than the boys. They were all intimidated, and she never had a date. Larry hung out with her, but those really weren't dates.

It all came back: the anger, the angst, and the chip on my shoulder. I raised my head, ready to bite hers off, but something in me sank like a stone, down into my stomach.

"You will be held after class in detention for one hour. I expect you to take the time to reflect on your attitude." Her voice brooked no defiance.

I lowered my eyes again, feeling them tear up. *What the heck?*

"Now, go to room one-oh-six for your detention duties."

# 8

I LEFT THE ROOM IN A FRUSTRATED SHUFFLE. It took ten steps to realize that my frustration, my anger at the unfairness of it all, wasn't me. Just to convince myself, I opened the Sight and looked back at the principal's office. Magick glowed greenish-white around the door. I couldn't make out exactly what, but based on my just-now experience, I was pretty certain that this angsty sensation had to be some kind of magick-based mental compulsion, or mental compliance.

Mind-influencing spells are illegal. The recipient's mind would immediately try to fight the compulsion, which created all sorts of mental trauma as the spell fought the resistance. People had been killed by the spell — making them walk in front of a car or killed by the brain hemorrhaging — because of the pressure from resisting the spell. If she was using that kind of magick, she was a felon. I had to find out before I accused her of anything.

Did she cast the spell? Or get someone to cast it? Or was it a residual spell placed on the room before she became the principal?

I was reasonably certain she'd cast the spell, but I wanted to confirm she was the caster. If she knew magic, and had enough power, then I could alert Dean, who could call it in.

Scratch that. My job had to be Ginny first, then the principal. I was being paid to get Ginny out of her family's abusive clutches. Do that, and then I could call in the cavalry. So, as much as I wanted to call Fawn, it was time to grit my teeth, be pragmatic, and take care of the job I was hired to do. I could use the Sight on the principal when she wasn't looking, and verify her as a spellcaster, then store it away and get Ginny.

I walked into the detention room. Ginny was there, along with two girls who wore letter jackets for Field Hockey. Both were large and stocky, reminding me of man-sized Trolls in a way, only without the green skin. They ogled Ginny as she cleaned the chalkboard (yes, they still use them).

As I stepped past the door, their gazes swiveled to me: the new target. One nudged the other, saying something I just couldn't quite make out. The two girls kept smiling as I sat down in the front row, as far from them as I could find a chair. Ginny finished cleaning the chalkboard, then grabbed a piece of chalk and began to write out a list.

"This is today's to-do list. I'm the student manager. So I'll assign work. You'll get it done and get on with the next job until the list is finished." She looked up, and her eyes widened, surprised at me being in the room. "When did you get here?"

"Just as you were cleaning the board."

I did it as mousy as I could, looking down at the desk quietly. Out of the corner of my eye I saw the two girljocks smirk at my reaction. I got the feeling they were going to try and corner me later. In high school, being small and inoffensive is a great way to get bullied by whomever. Those two looked like the bullying kind.

Ginny continued. "You, new girl. Please collect the trash bags on the west hall. Pat, you go to the maintenance room and move the sorted trash into the compactor. Frieda, you get to sort the trash bags and empty them into recycling or the compactor. I'll get the trash in the east hall. Any questions?"

No one said anything.

"Okay, get to it."

The two girljocks got up slowly, joking with each other. The sting of detention apparently didn't faze them at all. Ginny gave me a pair of thick rubber gloves and a push cart, like the ones used in hotels for luggage, and sent to pick up the trash bags. There were three types: green for recycled paper, red for biological items like food, and white for non-recyclable trash. The rack was big enough to get most of one side done before I had to go to the maintenance room.

Ginny finished up and pushed her cart down the east hall. "I'll lead you back. They won't do anything with two of us there."

She was a totally different person than what I expected. She was relaxed, comfortable and, for lack of a better description, together.

"What are those two in for anyway?"

Ginny continued pushing her cart. "They're on the Field Hockey team, if you didn't notice. They're both on defense, are the biggest girls in the school, and the biggest dykes in the school." She slowed her walking pace. "They both like to harass the other girls. They've been in detention enough that it's just another class to them."

I filed that tidbit of information away as Ginny turned her head to look back at me, stopping her cart.

"You're new. The Principal sent you here to read you the rules: Shape up, or else. Those three that cornered you? That's your welcoming committee. Vice Principal Villers' little pets. They're the Alpha clique. All of them have training in magick. The rest of the school doesn't. It's not taught here."

I tried not to give a too-wide-eyed stare at Ginny. "They know magick, and it's not taught here? Why not? Every school I've been in taught about magick and the dangers of it."

Ginny shrugged. "I think that's Mrs. Gross' call. She hates it, from what I hear, and only tolerates the three girls because Vice Principal Villers showed an interest in them." She turned back. "Stay away from them. They'll use magick to mess with the others, despite Principal Gross. Some girls got hurt because of it."

More information to think about. Which brought me back to a question of my own.

"So, like, why are you in detention? What'd you do?"

Ginny started pushing her cart once more. "I volunteered for it."

I stopped.

Ginny heard the cart stop, then stopped hers and turned to face me.

"What? You think I like being here? *pfft*. As if."

Attitude, sullen and black, rolled off her with a pressure I could feel on my skin. It didn't make sense. If she hated it here, then why did she volunteer? The answer came like a flash: She didn't want to go home. This delayed her trip back to her family prison for another hour or two.

I looked at Ginny again. My uniform, like most of the other girls, had a short-sleeved shirt. Ginny's wore long sleeves. Under her skirt, she wore the long dancer's togs, covering her lower body completely. That they were nearly identical with Ginny's pale complexion was why I hadn't spotted them before. Her face wasn't bruised, but the hate in her eyes at that moment convinced me that, like the reports had hinted, all was not right in the Cameron home.

Part of me wanted to just grab her right then and head out the back like my old plan: help her over the three-meter security fence, get myself over, and disappear into the woods until JC could drive to us.

I scrapped that idea again. *Too much time, too many people around, even if it was after school.* I would just have to bide my time and wait. This was only information gathering today. Despite my supposedly hardened exterior, something in me warmed to Ginny. Maybe it was high school all over again — kind of like *deja vu.*

We pushed the first load of trash into the maintenance area and dumped the bags in squares marked "Trash". The second pickup of the rest of the bags went by in silence.

I added up Ginny's actions: she hated her family, hated her situation, and probably hated this school. I couldn't blame her. Mrs. Gross and Mrs. Villers were not the matronly sort — more like prison wardens. People were throwing their unruly, entitled, spoiled children here, and then throwing money at the school to get them to fix their parental neglect. That was the impression I was getting from this place. Finally, detention finished, and Ginny had us sign a sheet, then she wrote a checkout time for each of us.

I walked out to the grungy PT Cruiser. JC picked was waiting. He gave me a polite bow, like a servant of a spoiled rich kid. He held my door open, closing it after I'd sat down, then got in the driver side, and we drove off towards my office.

"What'cha think, little boss lady?" He kept his eyes on the road as he spoke. "Is this all the real deal? Or a bunch of hot air in a barn?"

I scowled and slouched back in the seat.

"Now that is a fine little bit of acting, Fern. You look just like an angsty little teener."

I mumbled to myself and slouched deeper.

*Damn his know-it-all attitude.*

That sat me up. I focused inwards, doing my best to check myself. I couldn't feel any spell, but it was like I'd been in one. Maybe the spell was residual from the Principal's office? If it was, it was a strong one, and I should have picked up on that when I gazed at the office with the Sight. I hadn't, so that meant that I might have been a target of a spell? I had a while to think about it before we got back to the office, where I could test my theory.

It was a quiet ride back to my place.

Once back in the office, a quick test detected the slight *zing* of a spell breaking. I couldn't tell from who or what kind of magic, but I knew the effects. It was some kind of influencing spell. They're illegal, like I said before. That likely meant someone wanted something in that school that was worth the risk of discovery and capture by the RCMP.

I say "likely", because right now I was guessing. It made sense, but I've been wrong before. Still, a guess based on what you know is a reasonable start toward solving a mystery.

After mopping the floor, and erasing the circle, I brought JC up to date on what I'd found out.

He listened, occasionally straightening his tie. "As I understand it, Fern. You have a spellcaster in that school what isn't supposed to be there. A principal with an office that might be magicked in some manner, and a spell cast on you that can't be explained by the magick in the office? Is that about right?"

I nodded, a little flustered because JC sounded like Zhirk as he ticked off the points. A lump formed in my throat. It was unsettling how much JC acted like him.

"Well, as my pap always said, 'If you can't figure it out, go take a look and get your hands on the problem.'" JC chuckled.

"'course he was a mechanic, not a spell caster. Car problems are a little more physical and hands-on."

I nodded. He was right, though. We couldn't figure out what was going on until we were sure exactly what *was* going on in the Principal's office. Getting that magick identified might not help right away, but knowing what it was might give us more information to figure out this puzzle.

"I agree. Let's go back this evening. A little dark-of-the-night visit might get us something new."

# 9

I PULLED THE PT CRUISER INTO THE PARK across the street from the school and backed it carefully into a small copse of trees. Its dark color would help hide it from a casual glance, and set it up for a quick exit if, powers forbid, we had to leave fast. JC grabbed his guitar case. The chitters coming from it chilled my spine.

He noticed my reaction and chuckled. "Insurance in case we run into trouble." He patted the case and the eerie tittering ceased.

We loped from the car, across the street, to the front gate. I'd prepped for this back at the office and brought out the small bottle of oil. I whispered the words to release the magick and squirted the oil into the lock on the door, then onto the motor used to open and close the gate. The locking mechanism clicked as the bar rose, and the motor pulled the rolling gate open. JC and I listened for trouble. A place like this had to have some kind of security. I hadn't seen any cameras, but that just meant that the security would likely be of a more subtle nature. I guessed it would be more for inside the school than outside it.

JC took the lead. He carried two long lead bars about the length of my forearm in his right hand. His left hand clutched the guitar case. I quickly cast a counterspell on my hand. It was weak and unspecific, but it might just be enough if we came face to face with a hired spell-slinger.

We got to the front door without any incident. JC positioned himself at the bottom of the stairs, while I went up to the double front doors and used the oil can again. I discovered an electronic strip on each of the windows, which meant breaking them would set off alarms.

That was troublesome, but there were ways around it. I pulled out two small strips of paper, and held them in my left hand, using the right to feel along the edges of the doors. A light bump on the top right was where the door sensor had been mounted. I drew on both pieces of paper a pair of identical symbols, and then charged them with a spell.

This would act as a link on the two sensors, keeping both portions connected even when I opened the door. It's a tricky spell, but one that doesn't need a lot of time to prep or cast. You just have to keep your intent and focus.

Once I'd gotten the two pieces of paper set in place, I spoke the words to release the oil. The lock clicked open. More oil brought up the hand bolts, and it swung open silently.

I motioned JC up, and he took the lead, stepping in first. He paused, then waved me in.

"Slick little spell there. Where'd you learn it?"

I smiled and didn't answer. Hey, a girl's got to have a few secrets. Am I right? But between you and me, Larry has a surprising number of little tricks up his lanky sleeves.

Fortunately for us, the Principal's office was near the main entrance. We moved slowly towards the office, taking care to move as quietly as we could. I opened my Sight to look for any magick alarms that might be in place. I didn't see any, and the door looked the same as before: dark and bounded by an odd purplish light that was much more distinct now that it was dark.

Peering at the door, I couldn't find any magick traps or alarms. There weren't any electronic ones either. I dropped the Sight, and carefully squirted the oil into the lock and mumbled the release. The lock spun slowly, and the door opened with a light push. The office looked the same as when I was here earlier today: bookcases with old wrappers and magazines, a few with books scattered about.

I closed my eyes, and opened my senses. This close to a power source, my Sight could be more a hindrance than a help. A lesson to would-be magick-slingers: Don't open your Sight next to a magickal power. It's like facing a floodlight. I did it once. The pain was a harsh, but valuable, experience.

This place was old. That was the first thing that crossed my mind. There were myriad faint emotional traces of all kinds, mostly fear and trepidation. This was a Principal's office, after all.

As my senses expanded, that instinctive uneasiness started to shift. There was something like a whisper, but wasn't. It scratched at the edges of my self, quietly jeering, and saying that I was another rich, spoiled brat whom parents didn't love and just threw money at to keep distracted. Privilege and entitlement were nothing here. The only one that really understood me was Mrs. Villers. Mrs. Villers knew how hard it was to live in an unloving place. She was my one true confidant in a place of despair. *She was the one who cared, she was the one who knew ...*

JC shook me out of my daze. "Hey, Fern. You okay? You started drooling."

I blinked and shook my head to clear it. "I got what we were after. It isn't the Principal. It's the Vice-Principal. She laid a spell on the room. One to make the students see her as the one understanding person in the place."

JC grinned. "Oh, I like her. She's slick. Is the Principal in cahoots with her?"

JC rubbed his hands together, and that creepy guitar case wiggled as something inside gave an excited squeal and scratched quietly on the sides. He glanced at the case then back to me.

"What do you think she's doing that for? I can see all kinds of mischief," he rumbled quietly.

JC was right. Influencing minds was a devious shortcut to power. Power over someone's life — all of it. I wondered at how long the spell was in place. It didn't feel new. And how was it anchored? Usually spells faded over time unless recast. An office, especially one like this, would have people in and out all the time.

Coming in after hours, or staying late every so often, could cover the time needed to re-cast the spell. But doing it once and anchoring it on something made more sense. It was easier, and there was no adjusting schedules or making excuses to visit the school after hours or on weekends.

"I'd love to take this to the RCMP. If that happens, we lose a chance to get Ginny out of her troubles, and we weren't hired to sniff out a rogue magick-caster."

JC nodded, smiling. "Your call. You're the boss."

I didn't like it. But even the best intentions don't pay bills; a successful job does. I salved my conscience a little by promising myself I'd call Fawn after we'd gotten Ginny out. Until then, I'd do my best to stay clear of Mrs. Villers.

The next order of business was the school records. We'd come this far, getting a copy of Ginny's class schedule and records would help refine our plan. The records were in the main office, next to the Principal. Using the oil, we entered the office. Most records were kept online, so we would have to power up the computers, bypass the security code, copy the records, cover our electronic tracks, and power down the system, all without triggering alarms.

Yeah, not happening.

We went through the hardcopy files. Ginny's was last updated at the end of the previous semester, but her previous two years were in the file in detail, so we took pictures with JC's cellphone.

On a vicious whim, I looked for the teacher records. Ten minutes of rummaging around found them. They, like the students, were current to the last semester. Mrs. Gross' tenure stretched back fifteen years; Mrs. Villers' had been around for four years. Mrs. Villers was also the head of the after-school clubs, and, intriguingly, in charge of finding money and the lead in fundraisers for the clubs. JC took pictures of both her and Mrs. Gross' files, so we could peruse them at leisure later on. We took care in putting them back, trying to leave things as little disturbed as possible.

Once we finished straightening up, we snuck back out carefully the same way we'd come in. Using the spell on the oil, we re-locked the doors, and then pulled the paper strips and anything that might reveal we'd been here.

It was a much quieter ride back to my office. The responsible part of me was convinced that I was making a big mistake leaving Mrs. Villers free to continue her mind warping, but I had to think of my client and Ginny first. It's one of those choices where nothing is 'right', so you have to make a choice. I was hired to rescue Ginny.

I hated that I couldn't do both at once, but anything involving the school would likely put Ginny back in her parents' hands, and impossible to rescue. JC was much more about taking Mrs. Villers down, as to his mind leaving her loose would cause more trouble and we'd be morally responsible for any harm done. I agreed with JC, that Mrs. Villers was a threat as long as she was free, but she wasn't the job.

Mrs. Villers was simply incidental to our job, which was to get Ginny Cameron away from her toxic family. Ultimately, JC agreed that regardless of the potential threat Mrs. Villers posed, getting Ginny out was the priority. Then, if our consciences demanded (and we both knew they would), we'd work to expose her. I know I wanted to. I rubbed the nub of my finger and wished for the millionth time that Zhirk was around to talk to.

Zhirk would have known how to talk with me about this, and how to ease my guilt over leaving Mrs. Villers free to corrupt and control all those girls at Haven. It didn't feel right. I hated this feeling of being helpless to stop her. It was my choice, and I'd have to live with it. That's what being a professional is about – making the choice, and living with the consequences of that choice.

While I was brooding on the unfairness of having to make that call, JC was scanning Ginny's files.

"Oh here's something interesting. She's got an interest in French, and is in Forensics." He scrunched his brow. "What is 'Forensics'? Isn't that working with cadavers?"

"Forensics is like debate, but a bit more formal. It's a little more about the information behind the point, than an arguing for a change from a status quo."

"A what?"

I rolled my eyes and grinned.

"Debate is about making a speech about how and why something should change, or not change, depending upon the side of the debate you draw. It's really about persuading the audience to be on your side. Forensics takes it a step further. You are making the speech, but it is more about the how the speech is made, and the subject is much more flexible. Debate is arguing about, as one example, whether water should be drawn from a river, or left there." I smiled. "I took a debate class my senior year in high school."

JC nodded. "Okay, I follow that. So our girl's into public speechifying."

"Pretty much."

He shrugged and returned to reading. "Clubs give you a way to get close."

I nodded. "They do. I'll see about getting added to one of those clubs tomorrow."

JC nodded, then stretched, his hands nearly bumping the overhead fan.

"I'll get some rest, then likely enjoy the park after dropping you off. There's plenty of places to watch comings and goings at the school. Maybe I'll spot something we missed."

I nodded. "Good idea."

I went over to the Murphy bed, locked the file cabinets that served as its legs, then lowered it carefully.

JC got up and let himself out the front door. He waved, then closed the door behind him.

I flopped down on the bed. I think I was asleep before I finished falling.

# 10

T HE NEXT MORNING, I woke up tired and cranky. I hadn't had
but a few hours of sleep because of doing the 'break in and
snoop around' at the Haven School. It was raining, and the
forecast said it would turn into snow, with temperatures dropping
into the negative single digits.

Understand that here, on this side, with global warming,
any temperature in negative Celsius is cold, compared to what
really was cold before the Change, like negative thirty Celsius.
Snow is, at least here on the coast, a two to three times a year
event. Most of the snow doesn't last more than a few days.

I bundled up and grumpily sat in the passenger seat as JC
drove me to school in a newly rented Honda Accord. It fit in
better with the other cars. A bit on the inexpensive side, but hey,

it wasn't the slate grey, beat-up rolling disaster that the PT Cruiser looked like.

JC dropped me off at the front door, then went back to watch the campus from a secluded spot. He was there if, for whatever reason, things went pear-shaped and I needed a quick getaway. I walked through the front gate, and immediately ran into Mrs. Gross.

Spotting me amongst the other girls trotting quickly for the door, she stopped me in the rain and stared at me, crossing her arms in stern disapproval. I shuffled under her gaze, unwilling to look up and confront her.

"Your paperwork has not come through, Miss Holdwell. Remember, you only have a two-week's grace period." She leaned forward. "You may believe you are an entitled princess. But here, everyone is an equal. You will do your best in *each and every* class. This is when you set the pattern for the rest of your life.

"Your aunt is paying our fee to see that you get the best possible education for the future. Acting out, anti-social behavior, classroom antics, or anything deemed disruptive to a learning environment, *will be punished*. And it does not matter who your parents are, or who they know." She straightened back up. "Now go to your Home Room. It's far too wet and cold to be outdoors."

As I stepped away from Mrs. Gross, I caught sight of Mrs. Villers. She smiled softly at me, and I could feel the effects of a spell beginning to wrap itself around me. She was trying to get me ensnared in her mind magick!

At least that's what I thought. It's hard not to react when you know you're being attacked, and I almost lashed out at it. I gritted my teeth as I mentally resisted the spell, and considered whether to be outed as a trained magick caster, or let it hit and hope I could break it. I chose a third option and ran into the school, hoping distance or the loss of eye contact would break the developing spell.

Fortunately, it turned out that one or the other did work. As I got inside and out of her sight, the spell unraveled. This made me consider getting a "Don't notice me" spell set up for times like this. It would have to be specific, otherwise it would affect Ginny too, and make it harder to win her confidence. Then the thoughts about spells and strategy went on the back burner as the Home Room teacher began to call roll.

The classes went by like you'd expect: long, extremely detailed, and extremely boring. I watched the other girls. Most of them were either half-asleep or doodling in their books. One or two were paying attention. I didn't see any of the "magick clique" in the room, so I hunched down in my desk and tried to look for all the world like a surly, defensive, angsty teen while I opened my Sight.

I'd have rather just let my senses expand, but the instructor had been very diligent at catching sleepers the first day. I didn't want him to interrupt me and draw suspicion when I didn't respond. My Sight came up, and fortunately there were no practiced magick casters near me. Magick is like any muscle and skill: practice at it makes you better, and you can gather and hold more power. The more you do, the more you can do the next time, just like regular exercise.

What I saw was not unexpected. Everyone has magick talent to varying degrees, and most here were small, low-powered sorts that had barely scratched at it. They all glowed faintly in the sight, with a few girls surrounded by what looked like faint wisps of greyish-green fog. Was that the effect of Mrs. Villers? It was something to check on later. If I could watch Kinsey or one of the twins with the Sight, I'd be able to verify the "fog", since those girls were Mrs. Villers' favorites, according to Ginny. Hopefully, when I got the chance, it'd be at a distance, rather than so close I could tell what kind of mouthwash they used that morning.

The morning passed slowly and, by the end of the second class, I was fidgeting. I knew most of the stuff already. Most of the day was a review of basic information, so it wasn't hard to keep up. Sitting at a small desk for an hour made me restless. I was used to moving around a lot more.

When the lunch bell rang, I was up and out of the class before half of them were moving to get out of theirs. I went down the hall, looking for Ginny or the MC's ("magick clique", for you non-acronyminists). If I saw Ginny, I could ask her about clubs, since we had talked a little during detention. I could start working on getting her to trust me more, which would help when the time came to take her.

The MC's spotted me first. I was looking so hard for them I didn't notice them until they were right behind me.

"Oh look, it's Nine Fingers. How are you, dear? Getting your hand caught in a door?"

The setup was the same. Kinsey distracted me as the other two moved to make a triangle, with me in the middle.

"She looks nervous, J. What do you think we should do to help her relax?"

"How about finding her a place to sit, J? Oh poor thing, must be tired from all that walking on those short legs."

My legs were fine the way they were. They were just a bunch of bullies looking to put the "rules" to the new kid. I didn't need this; it wasn't worth the time of day. Why couldn't they pick on … I shook my head to clear it.

*Magick. It had to be magick.*

I focused on my own body. My feelings were my own, not what someone did to me. I watched Kinsey back up. Her eyes widened in surprise that I was putting up a fight instead of falling to the ground in despair.

The girls looked back to their right, and I saw Mrs. Gross clumping towards our little group like a bulldog cornering a rabbit.

"You four! Yes, you, Ms. Farren. Stay right where you are."

The girls froze like deer in a headlight. I saw Mrs. Villers behind Mrs. Gross, hurrying to catch up. Mrs. Gross got to us first.

"All four of you will be in detention after class today. Bullying is not tolerated here. And you, Ms. Cameron, you will learn to be a proper lady here, and not instigate confrontations like the one just I witnessed."

I wanted to stomp my foot and whine that it wasn't fair, which said that Mrs. Villers was trying to influence my actions and feelings. I ended up clenching my hands and staring at the floor as Mrs. Gross lectured me on proper etiquette in the school.

Once she finished, I turned my back to her and walked, trembling, to lunch.

The mood in cafeteria was, in a word, boisterous. Students went to the various stations where the white-uniformed and blue-aproned staff served up spaghetti, meatballs, hamburgers, baked potatoes, French fries, steamed vegetables, milk, and water.

The MC was at the center table, the three of them surrounded by hangers-on that wanted to be part of the "cool" group. I looked for one that was near a window so I could watch the sky. It might have been the lingering hints of the spell, but the table I chose was closer to the MC table than I actually wanted to be.

I'd gotten a burger and fries with water for lunch, not wanting a salad or the spaghetti. Institutional food, even at a school like this, never tastes good to me. Not in high school as a kid — and certainly not now. Fortunately, no one came to sit with me, so I could eat in peace.

I glanced over at the MC table, and saw Kinsey watching me. The little confrontation didn't go like she thought, and now I was

on her radar. *Great. Another complication that wasn't needed.* If
— when, I corrected myself — she decided to talk to Mrs. Villers,
the cat would be out of the bag about my being able to do magick.

Oh, not real magick, but focus like I used to break the spell
meant that I had more than the traditional amount of magick
training. And that would put me on Mrs. Villers' radar. It was
only two days into this plan, and it could be already unraveling.
I split my time between staring at my food, and gazing out the
window, as lunch went by.

After lunch, the classes dragged by like I was trying to walk
through a swamp. When the final bell rang, it was time to go to
detention — again. This time it was me, the MC, and Mrs. Villers.

I swallowed dryly. This was not good. Mrs. Villers controlled
the MC, and all four of them knew a little about mind spells.
Then Ginny walked in, and stood next to Mrs. Villers.

Mrs. Villers looked at Ginny as if she'd just bitten into
something bitter. "Ginny, why are you here?" Mrs. Villers voice
was soft as a light breeze.

I closed my eyes. My expanding sense could feel the brush
of magick. It wasn't directed at me, thankfully.

Based on my magick sense, Kinsey and the MC were to my
right and behind me; Mrs. Villers was in front. Mrs. Villers
magick swirled past me and towards where I remembered Ginny
was. It reached Ginny's location, where something like an
invisible wall stopped my senses. Mrs. Villers' power was rebuffed.

I opened my eyes to see her frowning at Ginny.

"Mrs. Gross wants to see you, ma'am. She said that you
hadn't collated the reports from last week, and she needs them
for accounting and inventory."

Ginny's voice was pleasant and neutral. She offered no
defiance, or angst. Just a simple girl, with a simple, but annoying
request from the Principal.

Mrs. Villers fumed for a moment, then turned towards the door, saying in a long-suffering voice, "That woman is so disorganized. Very well, Ginny, you are the detention monitor. I expect you girls listen to Ginny, and do what she says. I will see you for dismissal later."

She walked out of the room.

The MC deflated with their leader gone, and meekly accepted the assigned jobs for detention. Ginny had me collect trash while the girls did inventory of chalk and computer paper for each class. Where there was a surplus, it was shifted to the rooms short on material.

Ginny grabbed my cart, dragging it to a stop.

"What was that for?"

Ginny looked at me. "Two days you're here, and two days you're in detention. That's got to be some kind of record." She looked around. "Why was the bitch bunch all over you like that? They never go after the new kids. They make the crap roll downhill so someone else takes care of it." Ginny looked around. "I'm gonna trust you, 'kay?"

Trust? This was fast. It also made me wonder what was going through Ginny's head at the moment.

"Okay, I'll bite. What's going on?"

"You're wondering why I'm acting all weird after just meeting you twice in detention, right?"

I blinked. "Well, yeah. What about it?"

"Mrs. Villers is doing something to the kids in the school. It sounds crazy, but I think she's casting magick on them. They're all kinds of rebellious normal when they get here. Then they get thrown in detention by Mrs. Gross, and Mrs. Villers takes time off to meet with them personally."

I thought about this for a moment. That meant Mrs. Villers had a big operation at the school. The question was why.

I shrugged as Ginny left the statement hanging. "And?"

"And," Ginny continued, "then they're the same, but not. They don't push; they don't really hang out like regular kids. And everyone looks up to Kinsey and the twins."

"Looks up? You mean like they look at them like they're teachers?"

"Yeah. No one argues or crosses those girls. They all smile and gush about how great they are, which is creepy." Ginny looked up the hall. "We better get moving, we're a little late with the trash." She pushed her cart towards the maintenance room, and I followed suit.

When we came back for the rest of the trash, she whispered. "Don't let yourself get cornered by Mrs. Villers. She's the bad one, and Mrs. Gross just lets her do it."

"It makes me wonder why," I thought out loud.

"I don't want to know. They leave me alone; I leave them alone. I just want to get through school and get old enough to get away from home. I hate them."

"Hate them? Your folks?"

"Yeah, them. I'm not allowed outside after school, I have to do lessons on etiquette, lessons on who is who in the social pecking order. They want me to marry some jerk-off asshole that's the son of some huge, influential family." Her hands clenched into fists as her eyes began to fill. She angrily wiped her arm across her eyes and growled, "God, I hate it all! I hate it!"

I could believe that.

It sounded repulsive. Being forced to marry someone for political gain? It's the Dark Ages all over again.

"That's some seriously messed-up family, girlfriend."

Ginny looked sharply over as I spoke. She frowned as she said, "Girlfriend, huh?", and was the surly, suspicious teen I'd expected the first time I met her.

We pushed our carts to the maintenance room where the MC sorted the trash and dropped the non-recyclable stuff in the masher.

Ginny ran off before Mrs. Villers got back. I thought about it for a moment, then took off too. Being alone with the MC and Mrs. Villers was not a good idea at all.

JC picked me up out by the gate just as Mrs. Villers stepped out the doorway. She watched our car drive off, and the last glimpse I had of her was as she turned and disappeared back into the school.

"Anything new?" JC queried in his deep, honeyed voice.

"Yeah, and it's a doozy, if Ginny's to be believed."

JC's interest perked up and he gave his attention to the road. The explanation could wait until we got to my office.

When we got there, Sinera handed me a note. "Mrs. Thensome called, said that you'd been a bad girl at school." Her perfect Elven features scrunched up in a mischievous smile.

I called Mrs. Thensome while JC put his guitar case down on the ground. It chittered madly, drawing my attention from the call.

My throat went dry as he unsnapped the latches. "Please tell me you're not going to let that thing out!?"

JC looked up, amusement written on his craggy features. He paused dramatically, my eyes locked on his. I could hear Mr. Rich on the phone, asking who was calling. JC held my eyes for a long moment, Mr. Rich getting louder and less calm with each second. Then JC flipped the lid up, I gave a squeak and rolled the chair away from him as he reached in and pulled out a red acoustic guitar. He grinned, flipped the black strap over his shoulders, and started to tune it. Nothing chittered … or leapt at me with bared fangs. Just an Orc and his guitar.

"—swer or I will hang up the phone and block your number, Ms. Fat—" Mr. Rich's angry voice cut through my confused mind.

"Oh sorry, Mr. Rich. We had a little difficulty here. Taken care of. Mrs. Thensome called me. I'm returning her call."

Mr. Rich's tone went from smoldering mad to quiet efficiency in a heartbeat. "Thank you, Ms. Fatelli. I will inform Mrs. Thensome that you are returning her call."

A faint clatter came over the line as he put the receiver down at the other end.

Now you might think, with all the cellphones, home phones would be a dinosaur. Wrong, actually. Home phones are preferred. If you need help, the location is automatically known by law enforcement, who can dispatch officers to the scene in seconds. If you need help right away, they can translocate a team to the phone just by using the wire connection as a physical trace to the scene. A number of near-murders were prevented by that technique. It's become a literal life-saver.

"Ms. Fatelli, you are a very disruptive person. I've been called and requested to attend a meeting with Principal Gross to discuss details of your acting out and instigating self-attacks upon your person."

*Great. Like there wasn't enough drama at the school.* I'd better tell her about the spells.

"I think Mrs. Villers is using mind-magic on the students. Get yourself a protective spell against mental intrusion before you go to the school."

Mrs. Thensome was quiet for a long moment.

"Mr. Rich, please contact Mr. Kellen. I will have need of his services this evening." There was an indistinct murmuring in the background, then Mrs. Thensome sighed. "Of course, we will add in a bonus to his fee for the suddenness of the request." She then addressed me. "You will owe me a fee for this meeting. I'm to pay a fine for your actions." She paused for a moment. "Do you have anything else?"

"When is the meeting?"

"Promptly before school begins, so please show up a half-hour early. We will meet on the steps, and go directly to the Principal's office."

She hung up the phone without waiting for an answer.

# 11

THE NEXT MORNING, we were in the Principal's office precisely a half-hour before classes started. Mrs. Gross frowned at Mrs. Thensome for a moment, then a faint smile formed on her lips.

"Mary, it is good to see you here on the Haven campus once more. It's been fourteen years since we've had a chance to talk."

I looked between the two of them. Mrs. Thensome smiled thinly at me.

"I was the Valedictorian for my class when Mrs. Lucinda Gross took over for Ms. Grammist. How are you, Lucinda? I trust your charges are striving to meet the goals you expect of them?"

Mrs. Gross shook her squarish head. "This is not to be a pleasant conversation, I regret to say." She looked over at me.

"Your niece skipped her allotted time in detention, and I am afraid I must have her report each day for the next five school days. If there is a repeat, I will require you to pay a penalty fee of one-quarter of her tuition to the school and enroll her in Mrs. Villers' truancy adjustment class."

Mary Thensome looked over at me, a thin line of disapproval forming on her lips. "I hope you aren't going to be that troublesome, are you?"

She reminded me so much of Aunt Ruthie that it shocked me. I think I stared back at her, mouth open, for at least ten seconds before I shook off the uncanny resemblance in my head.

I shivered and replied, "No, ma'am."

Mrs. Gross lay her hands flat on the desk and studied the two of us.

"Your niece has learned the consequences of her disobedience, I hope. I do not wish a repeat of this situation."

"Neither do I," Mrs. Themsome replied levelly.

Mrs. Gross stood up, as did I and Mrs. Thensome. The two women shook hands, and then Mary Thensome walked me out to the lobby, where she drew me close like a mother hugging a daughter.

"I think you'd better not make that penalty fee happen. By my accountant's calculations, you've used up the estimated overhead expenses. Despite my wish to rescue this girl, there is a point of monetary no return. Keep that in mind, Ms. Fatelli."

I nodded, and said quietly as I stepped back out of the embrace, "I understand."

Then it was time to go to Home Room. I had the rest of the day to think about what had happened. The last thing I wanted was to get put in that disciplinary class headed by Mrs. Villers. That would be the one place where she could work on my mind without interference.

I knew for a certainty she could manufacture an incident that would get me assigned to that class, if I wasn't careful — and lucky. This now was about Ginny, and me.

I had three aces up my sleeve if trouble happened. One, I'm an adult. Though I might get arrested for falsifying my age, it would turn eyes on the school that Mrs. Villers didn't want. The second is that I am, however clumsy, a magick practitioner. I could see spells, and counter them if given a chance. Since getting back from PEI, where I fought the Elf lord Cobb, and possessed by the lingering spirit of Anolyn the Dragon, I'd found a few things out about myself.

I won't go into details here, but one advantage that grew out of that possession is I could cast without needing a circle and incantations. So yeah, now I could actually do combat magick. The third was JC and his guitar case. If a full-on fight brewed up, he'd be a juggernaut compared to the girls and the staff.

Me, the practical girl I am, wanted to avoid any kind of trouble. So with Ginny actually trying to help me stay out of Mrs. Villers' clutches, tomorrow or the next day would be the right time to move. It was actually a relief in a way to get back into classes. The make-work gave my mind a chance to concentrate on other things besides dodging the MC or Mrs. Villers.

When the lunch bell rang, and before stepping into the halls, I took a moment to focus my magick. I can't tell you how much a relief it is to not need a casting circle for every little spell. I focused the spell pattern in my mind and, a minute or so later, I stepped into the hallway and walked back to my locker.

The MC strolled by. One of the twins cast a glance in my direction, but didn't recognize me at all. They continued past me and turned right into the near hallway. I spotted Ginny, who waved back at me, which was a surprise. Only practiced mages would be likely to pick up that a spell was going on, and then they'd have to take a moment to identify what was tickling their senses. Ginny just looked unaffected.

She walked over to me. "Lucky they missed you, eh?" She straightened her uniform and leaned close to whisper. "They're not going to give up until Mrs. Villers gets hold of you and turns you into a ..." she air-quoted, "... 'model student'."

All I could do with the obvious was nod and grimace.

"So why not 'out' her? Sic the cops on her? Something."

Ginny stared at me, her mouth curling into a frown. "I do that and the school closes, I go home, and now, without a school to stop it, I get forced to marry some cement-head just so my folks can get more political connections. If she goes, I go. That's the sucky part."

"Why not just run away?"

Ginny looked at me like I'd just asked the dumbest question she'd ever heard.

"I can't."

"Why not?"

"I just can't. Okay?!" She turned towards the lockers. "I got a tracker under my skin."

"Say ... what?" I stood flabbergasted at Ginny's big reveal. *A tracker? What the hell?*

"Yeah, one of those tracker things they put in dog's ears. They said it was to keep me from being kidnapped, but they did it after I ran away the second time. They want to find me anywhere I am, at any time. I'm just the freaking pet bitch dog they get to give away to some dumber-than-dirt stud, so I can get my folks all the money they can spend."

She clenched her hand like she was going to punch the locker, then sighed dramatically and let her hand drop.

"Who am I kidding? They got my life planned for me and this stupid tracker makes sure I can't get away. It's all screwed up."

This was the biggest gift to drop in my lap I could have hoped for. She wanted away from them *and* had a problem I could fix.

I wondered again if magick was arranging things for its own benefit, but decided not to look such a gift horse in the mouth. If this was given to me on a silver platter, I was sure as heck going to use it!

"So you're wanting out?"

I tried to sound nonchalant, but my own eagerness might have leaked out, as Ginny suddenly gave me a very hard, probing stare. She held it for a few moments, then relaxed.

"Exactly. I want out. I want the freedom I see everybody else having. I want to choose. I want the freedom."

"Don't we all."

I knew that as a teen, I'd wanted that very thing. What I had to learn was that freedoms are bound by rules themselves.

If you want to throw everything away and live by your own rules, you had to do it outside of society. Serial killers, for example, can't just walk into town. They're bound by their rules for choosing victims. They have to find the next one, regardless of the perceived risk. Not finding one means a reward delayed, and someone with such little self-control hates waiting for anything.

Those that do evade capture are usually living the life of the homeless: moving around constantly, with nothing to show for their efforts but dead bodies. I'm really over-generalizing, I know.

Teens have wants and needs that at times are still hard to define, or understand — even to themselves. Right now, Ginny wanted freedom — freedom from her parents to make her own rules. I could use that to get her to come with me and get her out, just like she wanted.

All I had to do was to arrange an escape.

# 12

AFTER TALKING WITH GINNY, I kept the "Don't notice me" spell up. It was easier to maintain a spell than to constantly re-cast it. As a result, the rest of the day went pretty smoothly. I had to report to detention, but wanted to make certain Mrs. Villers wasn't there. She was. So was the MC. All four magick-slingers in one place. Mrs. Villers certainly didn't let grass grow under her feet. Time for another change of plans.

I hung out away from the detention room and waited for Ginny. I dropped the "Don't notice me". It would be too difficult to do the next things if I had to maintain a spell during a quick casting. The sound of approaching steps got my attention. It was Ginny, but she was heading the wrong way. I focused and attempted to recall what I'd seen about her schedule. The answer came to me immediately: today was French Club. That was why Mrs. Villers was in the detention room.

I had to be quick, or they'd see me in the hall. It was about time to report in and start serving my punishment. I ran up behind Ginny, who turned as she heard my pounding feet.

"What the? Wha—"

I didn't try to explain, I just grabbed her wrist and pulled her with me into the cross hall. Ginny didn't like the rough treatment, but sensed there was something big going on. She went back to the corner and looked down the hall, then came quietly running back to where I was in the Science lab.

"Okay, what's going on? I thought you'd be gone in detention."

"Never mind that. You said you had a tracker on you? Do you know where?"

Ginny blinked as I asked the question. "What?"

"Where is the tracker?"

Her lower lip started to push out. She was getting stubborn with me running roughshod over her. She wanted answers.

"Come on, Ginny, tell me. I can break it so it doesn't work." I held my hand out and conjured up a small flame.

Ginny's eyes widened. She looked at me, mentally putting two and two together.

"Between my shoulder blades, next to the spine. They wanted it where I couldn't cut it out."

She turned and pulled her shirt up, exposing her bare back. "It's just above my bra strap."

I focused and looked at Ginny's back. Footsteps in the hall got louder as either Mrs. Villers or one of the MC checked the rooms. That spurred a rising sense of urgency. If she saw us, I didn't want to guess at what would happen. Just go with worst case and try to avoid it, Zhirk would say.

"Bite down on something," I told her.

Ginny pulled her shirt up, and stuffed a wadded up corner in her mouth as I pushed my fingers on the tracker under her skin to get an idea of its size. It was bigger than I expected, about the size of a dime.

I focused and sent tendrils of power to the lump. I could sense the electric power of a battery in the device, which meant I'd have to be careful. Using magick to break it would cause the corrosive chemicals to leak out. Heating it to damage it would hurt Ginny. The best way would be to pull it out, which would hurt — a lot. I had to swallow back a wave of nausea.

The thought of the pain had me thinking of Cobb, and how Kent and Kevin had screamed as he tortured them. I gritted my teeth and forced myself to focus on the here and now. This was not the place for scattered thoughts – or impromptu surgery.

"Forget it," I said to Ginny. "This won't work here. Follow me, and we'll get out off the school grounds first."

Ginny slid her shirt back down, and we moved to the far corner of the room, away from the open door. Kinsey poked her head in and did a look around. I'd gotten my "Don't notice me" up again. She mumbled a spell of her own. Crap. I gritted my teeth and hoped my spell would outdo hers.

I knew I was stronger, but it's stupid to discount luck. Any little thing can trip you up. Fortunately, she walked past, unable to sense us, and moved on to search the next room. As her footsteps receded, we both let out the breaths we'd been holding.

"Okay, we go out the fire exit. Tripping the alarm will confuse things. We'll take that time to get to my car, and we'll get out of here."

I started to get up, but Ginny pulled me down.

"Are you nuts?!" she whispered fiercely. "Your folks will just turn me over. It'd be kidnapping if they didn't."

I shrugged. "I know. I'm not going to detention. I don't like Mrs. Villers or her girl crew. The best thing's to run. We do that; this gets investigated. We can put the screws to Mrs. Villers."

Ginny thought about it for a few seconds.

"Let's get out of here."

I peeked out the doorway. The hall was clear.

Ginny and I moved as quietly as we could out of the Science lab down the hall, away from the main doors. We got to the fire exit without being seen.

"Okay, follow me and look for an Orc all dressed in black. He's our ride out of here."

Ginny nodded. "You sure you can get rid of the tracker? I don't ever wanna go back."

I nodded as I looked back down the hall, alert for movement.

"You ready? Now, or never."

Ginny nodded, and we pushed the door open.

Immediately, the fire alarm went off. Just under the noise of the blaring wail of the horn I could hear confused shouts back down the corridor. We sprinted out, then turned towards the street. I hoped JC was parked where he always was.

As we turned the corner and ran towards the fence, I yelled out, "JC! Get the fence!"

JC looked up from his guitar he had been noodling on. I thought I saw him mouth "Oh hell", and slid the guitar into the open window, then walked to the fence as we charged up.

"What're you doing?! Stay right there! Raise your hands!"

The RCMP were right on the spot. They had JC cold. Ginny's chauffeur had armed himself with an assault rifle of some kind and stayed behind the officers, who covered JC with their pistols braced.

*Crap.* It was improv time.

I skidded to a stop and screamed at the top of my lungs.

"FIRE! There's a fire in the building! Get help! Oh, please hurry! They're trapped!"

The RCMP hesitated.

JC smiled. "I'm not going anywhere officers. That's my charge there."

"Please hurry! They can't get out!"

I was screaming for all I was worth, and Ginny joined in. That settled it for the cops, and they darted towards the front doors.

There came an outraged squawk from the fire doors as Mrs. Villers came trotting out and spotted us. JC put two and two together fast — faster than Ginny's chauffeur. He charged the man who'd turned to watch the officers. JC flattened him like a runaway truck, knocking him four meters back towards his vehicle. Ginny and I sprinted for the gateway and charged through as Mrs. Villers tried to make herself heard above the fire alarms. JC escorted the both of us back to the car, then got in and peeled out. We left in a hurry and I had Ginny turn to face away from me.

"Bite down on a wad of your shirt. This is going to hurt."

Ginny nodded, and pulled her shirt up, bunching a hunk of it and sticking it in her mouth once more.

I focused on the spot, drawing power. While JC drove, I got my lipstick out and drew a fast and sloppy circle around the tracker.

JC kept glancing back in the rear view mirror. "What are you tryin' to do, Ms. Fatelli?"

"I'm going to get this tracker out from under her skin." I glanced at the rear view mirror to see JC's face.

"Well, that sounds like a good plan, but I think this'll work faster." He shifted his weight, then handed back a double-edged fighting knife. "Watch the edge, I use it to shave. It's good an' sharp."

I gingerly took the knife and used my finger to locate the tiny tracker again.

Ginny was pale, breathing rapidly. She shivered visibly, her eyes squeezed shut. If she was frightened of sharp objects, I wondered about how safe this idea was going to be.

I settled for a compromise. I put the dagger on the floor, then finished the circle around the tracker. Satisfied I could use the circle, I had to brace suddenly as JC took a corner at speed.

When he straightened the car out, I asked Ginny, "Are you ready?"

"Just get it done."

I took that as a "yes". I picked up the knife, got my cigarette lighter from my school bag, then heated the blade on both sides to sterilize it. Then I concentrated and focused power into the circle. Ginny and I braced as JC took another hard corner, then slowed down.

"No one's following, so we'll take an easy ride back home," JC announced.

Thank god for that. I recast the power into the circle, visualizing it expelling the tracker. When it started to stretch Ginny's skin, I slid the knife parallel to her back. She whimpered. I pushed fast.

The knife was as sharp as JC had said, cutting Ginny's skin like tissue paper. She screamed through the sodden mouthful of shirt as the tracker came popping out of the cut like pus from a lanced boil.

I grabbed the tracker and rolled the window down, throwing it out of the car.

*Let 'em follow it now.*

I fed more power into the circle, using it to slow the blood flow escaping from the cut. I undid my shirt after it had slowed, and pressed it against the wound.

"JC, how soon until we get home? I want to butterfly this cut closed."

"Almost there."

The car lurched as smooth cement gave way to crumbled, uneven asphalt. We'd pulled into the parking lot of my office. Ginny had stopped making noises, but had trouble standing. JC scooped her up, and the three of us hurriedly went upstairs.

Once we were back in my office, JC put Ginny on the Murphy bed. I rolled Ginny to her stomach, and finished the job on her back, slathering it with antibiotic, and using butterfly tabs to hold the wound closed. I got some alcohol to remove the lipstick circle. Ginny yelped at the sting of the cold alcohol as I cleaned her back.

While I worked on Ginny's back, JC made the call to David Cameron. We'd gotten Ginny out. Now it was time to finish the job, and get paid.

I got Ginny a shirt and sweater from my old clothes. She looked at them dubiously, me being a bit smaller and thinner than she was. Ginny tried a few of them on slowly. The old clothes fit a little snug, but well enough. Soon, she was out of her School Dress and into baggy blue jeans, one of my "band" shirts, and a deep blue sweater. She nodded at Sinera as the Elf entered my office.

Ginny turned her gaze to me. "So, now what do we do?"

She had a pensive look like everything had gone so well that she was waiting for the other proverbial shoe to drop and screw everything.

I offered her a chair and then sat down at my desk.

"Now, we wait for your uncle to come pick you up."

Ginny blinked. "My uncle? My folks never told me about any relatives. I figured I didn't have any." She fidgeted in the chair. "Is he really my uncle?" Her posture said loads about suspicion and distrust of the man's intentions.

I faced her, and gave her the facts as I knew them.

"The best I can tell he is. The tax department doesn't exactly keep things like genealogy on the forms."

I got back up and walked to her, placing what I'd hoped was a reassuring hand on her shoulder. "He paid me and JC to get you out of there."

I pulled her file from the bent filing cabinet and handed it to her. She looked through the information.

"Is he an okay guy?"

I thought about the question. "I think he's a pastor. He sounded all right. He was, umm, a little excessively earnest about things, and especially about your welfare." I shrugged as I gathered my thoughts. "I guess kind of like a car salesman pastor. A little slick. Not bad slick," I amended hastily, "Just slick like he'd been talking to people all his life."

Ginny nodded. "A used car salesman pastor uncle." She allowed herself a small, hopeful smile. "It can't be any worse than home was." She fidgeted in the chair. "How did he find out about me? I mean, my folks built that mansion so they could shut out the world."

"That, I don't know. It'd be a good question to ask him when you have time." I turned to JC. "Could you get the television? With as big an exit as we made, I want to know what the RCMP is saying."

JC nodded, then walked over to the small flat-screen TV I'd placed over the new brick by the windows. He turned it on. The screen was on Channel 6, which was Halifax's local station. The big news was, surprisingly, not us.

We were a distant number three on the list after a report of some "Children of Humanity" attack on a Fae section of town. They'd apparently torn through the area on a concerted drive-by that included grenades (both thrown and launched), automatic weapons fire, and, most horrifically, a gasoline truck with two mounted flame throwers. They'd lit a whole neighborhood on fire before crashing and going up in a fireball of jellied fuel.

Second was the attempted assassination of the Mayor of Halifax, James MacDonald, by members of a Fae fringe group calling themselves "Horn of Justice". Four of the sixteen-member council died in the assassination attempt. All the Fae died, most by the RCMP; some by their own hand.

After those two lurid incidents, a girl disappearing from Haven High School had no "wow factor" for television. Ginny was the first to break the silence after hearing the mind-numbing news.

"What happened? Did everyone decide to take a crazy pill today?"

JC looked over at me. "I think the girl is more right than wrong. The whole place is upside down with all this. Who tries to kill a Mayor and the whole council, which is over half Fae? And a Fae fringe group at that?" He shook his craggy head. "Who in their right minds would do that? I never even heard of any Fae banding together like that."

We were a very unsettled trio when the phone rang. JC turned off the TV while I answered the phone.

"Fatelli, Investigations."

Cameron's voice was a lot smoother over the phone. "Hello, Ms. Fatelli! It's so good to hear from you. I'm sure Ginny is doing well and has a lot of questions. How about we meet up somewhere outside of Halifax? With all the chaos on television, I'd feel better if we met away from where the trouble, or overzealous attention could happen."

I couldn't argue with the suggestion. Getting out of town where both the bad guys and the RCMP are going to be trigger-happy sounded like a good idea to me.

"Sounds good. Where should we meet?" I didn't exactly like the idea of doing things by his direction, but he was the client, so I made allowances.

"Do you know that small bump in the road called East Preston?"

I closed my eyes and mentally visualized it on a map.

"Yeah, it's near Lake Eagle, right? East of Halifax a little way."

He chuckled. "That's exactly right. I'll meet you at the Holy Light Church there just north of East Preston on Graveller Road."

I nodded. "What time?"

I thought he had a time already chosen, but he surprised me slightly by saying, "What time would you think best to bring Ginny out here?"

I gave that some thought.

"How about tonight, around six pm? It'll be quiet, and I don't think we'll have any trouble getting there."

"Six o'clock it is, Ms. Fatelli. I'll be seeing you then."

Time to remind him why he was a client. "And my fee? I have a few bills to pay."

His silence wasn't surprising. I think most clients would prefer to forget my substantial fee. I mentally ticked off six seconds before I heard his honey-smooth voice reply.

"Of course, Ms. Fatelli. I'll have a check made out to the agreed-upon sum. And again, thank you. You don't know how much having Ginny free of that toxic household means to me."

That statement, for some reason, didn't sound at all like what I think he wanted it to. It set off a little alarm bell in the back of my head. I put it off as being keyed up after the kidnapping. It wouldn't hurt to have insurance, though. I'd bring JC along. I hung up the phone and turned to Ginny and JC.

"You're going to see your uncle tonight. We'll be taking you to the meeting place at six. JC, would you mind riding along on this one? I wouldn't mind company to chat with on the drive home."

JC nodded. "That would be a fine idea. We can celebrate."

The guitar case in the corner chittered and rocked enough to fall down, which made all of us go silent.

"I do believe that could be called an omen," JC mumbled.

It turned out that it may well have been.

# 13

WE GOT TO THE CHURCH RIGHT AT SIX. And I should have seen things coming a mile off. I think I did, actually, but I didn't want to believe it. Kent and Kevin were gone; we'd buried them a month ago. The wounds hadn't had but the barest time to scab over. I found myself drifting on occasion, wishing the past could be changed.

It can't. The past is set in stone, and the future is all smoke and mirrors. The present, the now, is where that smoke and mirror image become solid with the tick of a clock. Time has a magic all its own. But it takes time to ease sharp pains and make them dull. It takes time to grieve.

I'd thrown myself back into work as a way of not sinking into despair. I kept myself busy, without time to think about all the losses, all the death. Yeah, I was trying to escape the grief, and pushing so hard to escape it, that my reactions spilled over into this job. Sometimes that drowned out my little inner voice, which was trying to tell me to pay attention.

A single vehicle sat near one burned-out overhead lamp. It looked a lot like a variant of the old Hummer that the armed forces still use. Its light color revealed itself to have a pearlized finish in our headlights. JC stayed in the back seat while Ginny and I got out. Ginny was still in my sweats and band shirt, having decided that she didn't want to wear that school uniform one more moment.

The Hummer look-alike disgorged four people, which immediately set my hackles up. I didn't like the idea of being outnumbered, but no one had set numbers for either side, so it may have just been a precaution on Cameron's part — or so I told myself. After all, with all the crazy that had gone on in the news, precautions weren't a bad idea. That's why JC was in the car and, hopefully, out of sight.

The four approached me and finally got close enough get into the light. Cameron was there, along with three Hamref that looked like they belonged at an outlaw biker rally. All three wore black leather pants, a sweatshirt with the arms cut off, and a thick leather sleeveless jacket. I could see knives hung at their hips, and one looked like he had a boot knife as well. My hand slid into my purse, finding the snubnose. I gripped it and hoped I wouldn't have to use it.

The Hamref started to fan out into a semi-circle. Cameron stepped forward and greeted me with a smooth smile.

"Ms. Fatelli, I really appreciate all that you've done for Ginny and myself. I was in the depths of despair to hear of my niece's terrible suffering in that loathsome household. My brother-in-law never had his heart in raising her properly, or giving her a home full of warmth and love."

I wondered when he'd get to the point. I only half-listened, keeping my eyes on the three Hamref, who noticed my attention and froze, just like predators waiting for the prey's attention to slip. Not this time.

"So why the bodyguards? This doesn't look like a friendly family gathering."

David Cameron smiled. "It's not, actually." His hand was in his pocket.

Ginny spoke up. "Just what the hell do you think you're doing? What is this?"

Cameron, if that was his real name, paused. The Hamref didn't. They swarmed me, tackling me to the ground. I scratched and bit anything I could, terrified I was going to die. Ginny screamed, then I heard a thud.

One of the Hamrefs disappeared, leaving the other two to finish me off. I think my small size worked against them. Their knives sliced my thick jacket to pieces, but fortunately missed me.

I heard the sounds of a car door opening. JC had gotten out of the car. Then came a maniacal chittering that froze my blood. The Hamref and I both froze as the chittering rose in volume. I could just see past one of the Hamref. JC had the case open and held a spindly thing that my eyes didn't — or maybe more accurately, couldn't — focus on.

He dropped it on the asphalt and said, "Sic 'em."

The spindly thing chittered and shrieked as it scampered across the parking lot like a demented four-legged spider. I couldn't scream; I couldn't move. The hideous noises the creature made paralyzed me with fear.

It had the same effect on the Hamref. JC wasn't affected. I noticed white wads of something in his ears. He'd plugged them with cotton! Suddenly, the Hummer look-alike roared to life. Its four wheels churned on the pavement as the driver hauled the car around and roared past me, JC, and the paralyzed Hamrefs, disappearing down the long drive and into the night.

The creature shrieked again and shambled on sticklike legs towards me. My mind nearly went white with terror as it pounced on the first Hamref. A delicate beak unfolded from under its head and locked forward. The end looked razor-sharp. A drop of fluid fell from the end. The pavement hissed as the liquid splashed on the asphalt. It leaned over, using the beak to probe at the Hamref's face and shoulders. It shifted lower, then plunged downward into the Hamref's neck, piercing it.

The Hamref shrieked, then shuddered. A few moments later, its feeble thrashing stilled, then its body began to shrivel. The chittering thing held onto the withering Hamref with its two spindly front legs. Its body expanded slowly as it sucked the Hamref's fluids, like drinking a thick shake through a straw.

The second Hamref tried to throw off the effects of the paralyzing sounds, slowly rolling to its side. The thing pulled its beak free of the empty husk of the first Hamref and shrieked. My overloaded brain couldn't take the renewed terror. I passed out.

JC was kneeling next to me when I finally woke back up.

"How are you feeling, bosslady?"

I looked up at JC, then screamed and backed up as I spotted the guitar case next to him. The bone-chilling chittering started up, then quit when JC gave the guitar case a tap with his foot. I think my eyes were too big for my face as I stared at that guitar case.

"What was that?! What the hell was that?!"

The only reason I didn't pull my snubnose pistol was that I was so frightened that I'd forgotten about it.

JC smiled patiently, and waited until I calmed down.

"How about we start over?" He offered me a huge yellow-green hand to help me up off the ground.

I warily took it, not taking my eyes of the guitar case. "It's not going to get out?"

JC chuckled in that rich deep voice of his. "In a word: no. Its home is in that case. So it's not going to leave there unless I ask it to." He smiled disarmingly, which is a real trick. Orcs, as a general rule, always look like you owe them money ... and you're overdue.

"What is that thing, JC? Oh crap! Ginny! Where's Ginny?"

I knew the answer even as I formed the words. My memory was clearing, and the scream as Ginny was grabbed reminded me that, scared or not, Ginny had been forcibly taken. That the new kidnapper was my client was salt in my wounded pride.

"Where did the truck go?"

JC pointed north. "That way, though I don't know if they stayed going that direction." He shrugged. "That's just the way they left the lot."

"Thanks for the save, JC. They'd have gutted me if you hadn't sent that ... thing after them."

"You're truly welcome, Ms. Fatelli. After all, neither of us has been paid. And since you're my boss, I think you need to talk to that Mr. Cameron. I'm afraid that I'm not very good at interpersonal things."

JC straightened his suit jacket, then picked up the guitar case. "Shall we go back to the barn and decide what our next move is going to be?"

That was a good idea. If we wanted to come at this without getting killed, a plan would be needed.

"I'd rather go right in and take her back, but that's kind of a bad idea."

I thought for another moment. Cameron knew we weren't dead, so he would expect that we would try to get Ginny back. Not because she'd been kidnapped, but because as the person hired to get her out of trouble, I'd taken a responsibility for her safety. Cameron blew all of that away when he tried to kill me. There was Ginny — and my pride as a professional — on the line here.

I get a person I'm contracted to get out of danger killed; that puts a huge blemish on my record. My fault or not, I saw it as survival. If I wanted to get more jobs, I had to correct this one. That brought up another question.

"JC, what, exactly, is that thing in your guitar case?"

"You're not going to let that go, are you?" He sounded not exasperated, just … resigned.

"How can I? I saw it up close and personal. I saw what it did to that Hamref." A lump formed in my stomach. "It's … an Outsider, isn't it?"

"Honestly, I'm not certain. I don't think it is. The man who owned this guitar case before me got it from someone else, who didn't know what it was. I just call it 'Mack'. Its home is in the guitar case. Though why someone put it there is way beyond my understanding. What I do know, is that it is smart. It instinctively knows who's a friend, or an enemy. I've never had to tell it anything; it just knew." He shrugged his thick shoulders, then had to straighten his coat again.

"So that thing does know who the enemy is?" I looked at the guitar case, which chose that moment to chitter and rock.

JC tapped it with his boot and it quieted once more.

"Yes, indeed. It's never attacked anyone I didn't tell it to, nor has it hurt anyone around me that I didn't want hurt."

As much as I wanted to believe that, I didn't want to test it.

"Let's get back to the office."

I rubbed the nub of my missing finger, and wondered what Zhirk would have said about a thing like that.

# 14

AFTER WE GOT BACK TO THE OFFICE LATER THAT NIGHT, it was time to put our heads together and come up with a plan. JC suggested extra people. I wasn't sure I wanted others in on this, but having extra people meant more things could get done faster — and safer. The downside was more people meant a greater chance of things getting screwed up. It would have to be small group to keep noise down. I mulled over who would be best to ask.

Two people I did not want to involve were Fawn and Larry. Fawn wasn't showing yet, but it was barely the end of her first trimester. No, I especially did not want to see my sister in the middle of this. That, and she was still a cop. What we were planning, however justified, is still kidnapping in the eyes of the law — yet another good reason not to include Fawn or Larry.

"What about that fella you asked for help before? The other private investigator?"

"Dean?"

"Yeah, that's the name you mentioned before."

That made sense. Dean Youngwood was smart, and knew what he was doing. He made sense to include in this.

"I'll ask him, but I'm not getting my hopes up," I told JC. "He's pretty straight arrow, so something like this he might say no to, however noble the cause."

JC shrugged. He leaned over and snapped open the guitar case. I flinched away, putting my hand on the big glass ashtray on my desk. He reached in, pulling out the battered old red-fronted guitar. He closed the case with a tap of his foot, and began idly strumming the strings. I think I started breathing again when the case shut.

"You know, we don't even have a clue where she is. That's going to be number one on the list: 'Find the girl.'"

I nodded. "Find the girl, and find out what's waiting. I think it's a safe bet he knows we're still alive."

JC nodded. "I'm sure he does. Which means he might be shoring up his defenses, and trying to decide the best way to take us out. He knows where you live, after all."

JC glanced at the glass door to my office, with its large gold letters proclaiming that behind this door was "Fatelli Investigations".

"Point taken. And while waiting for him to show would be nice, I don't think he'll accommodate us by being stupid."

JC chuckled, then replied, "I suppose not, which means this is gonna be like a treasure hunt."

I had started to lay things out and, while we didn't know anything about where, we could do more research on *who*: namely, David Cameron.

"I'll give Dean a call about this. He doesn't have to get involved; he just has to do a little digging while we work on some other ways to find …"

Inspiration hit. I still had Ginny's school uniform! We had a way to find her!

"JC, clear things to the walls. I'm going to do a casting."

Between JC and I, it took only a few minutes to push the chairs and the desk to one side, opening up the center of the room. I wished I could pour a silver circle, but the landlord wouldn't allow it. And, despite what you think, landlords that put up with stuff like what's happened over the last three months are hard to find. I liked my office, and wanted to keep it, so chalk and powdered silver it was.

Once the circle was done, I got Ginny's clothes, and thanked my lazy habits of bundling laundry for the end of the week. Personal items are powerful components for personalized spells, like a tracking one. Again, I didn't need to go through the chanting to call up power in the circle. I could draw it through me and direct it mentally into the circle. Whatever that dragon did to me had sure boosted my spell casting. Possession by Dragon: the guaranteed way to increase magick ability. Yeah, and the moon is made of green cheese. I never, never, never, want to go through that again.

A half-hour later, we had our tracker. For convenience's sake, I put all of her clothes into a large plastic bag to make it easier to carry. The school uniform was large, but being intact made the spell stronger, which means it had a greater range. We didn't have to be as close as I had to be with Ahiah/Baldy when we used a piece of his shirt to track him.

Figuring now that Cameron and his cronies would be waiting for us, we had an alternate way of finding the location. We would drive around until we get a hit, then note the direction. Then we drive to a point away from the first and see where the tracker pulls. Mark the two locations, and the directions that the tracker pulls up on the map. Where the lines cross will be where Ginny is. That way, we don't have to see her to find her, and no one shoots guns or spells at us.

We got a hit five minutes out from the office, driving towards Lake Echo. JC pulled over, and I used a compass to get an exact reading and put it down on the map. Then we drove perpendicular to our previous direction of travel.

The one thing that's tough about this "new" magick casting is that it wipes me out more than the old method. I must be using some personal energy besides what I drew upon from the environment.

It took a while to get another hit. We were apparently right at the edge of its effective range. I repeated the process and drew the second line. It crossed the first line at a blank spot on the road map.

"Ms. Fatelli, I believe we are gonna do some backpacking."

JC grinned and tapped his knuckles against the guitar case he had nestled up against the back of the passenger seat. I couldn't help it, I shivered. That thing – that … Shambler, I decided to call it — was terrifying. The way the Hamref collapsed as the Shambler sucked it dry still made me want to vomit.

We drove back to the office, and I cleared space on my desk to spread the map out. JC set his guitar case next to the guest chair, then sat down to look the map over. Little scraping noises came from the case until JC gave it a tap with his foot. That brought the horrifying images of the Shambler up once again.

To throw off the disturbing thought, I sat down at my big oak desk and started to doodle out ideas and words at random, trying to see what the next steps would be, trying to anticipate what Cameron had done, and was going to do.

Why the breakneck pace?

Simple.

The first twenty-four hours in any police case are the most critical. It's when everything is still fresh in the minds of witnesses. It's the time needed for a felon to make tracks and get outside of a potential dragnet. It's the time needed for a serial killer to move a victim to a prepared site for killing, and have time to show up at his job without raising suspicion — provided he is working steadily.

There were a lot of reasons, but the main one was more selfish: I wanted to save my reputation. I knew Cameron was trouble, and yet I had still gone along with his requests. It was my responsibility. So I saw it as my job to clean up my mess. Doesn't that sound dramatic?

It was to me, now that I look back on it. I got that stupid White Knight attitude: that I had to be the only one to make a screw-up right. Real life isn't about being the only one. It's about taking the responsibility, and making sure you've got the right stuff for the job you plan to take on.

So, we decided to drive out there at night, look the place over, take a few pictures, and then see what we could make of the situation. Ginny was out there, and held against her will. That Cameron went through all this work to get me to do his job meant he had something important invested in her.

The most dramatic thing I could think of was some kind of sacrifice, like a virgin to appease a volcano god — which we, in what was left of Old Canada, thankfully, don't have. There were plenty of things out there that would love a sacrifice, but the question became: Why Ginny? What was so special about her that required all this elaborate planning?

A plan like this is about diversion. If you can divert attention from the true manipulator, you can stop any follow-up investigation in its tracks. Which made sense why he'd tried to kill us. We disappear. Ginny disappears. And no one knows who or what to look for. I'd left a loose end, though: Dean.

I'd asked him to dig up Ginny's records. If Cameron was smart, especially in an operation like this, he'd have someone, somewhere, looking at how to wreck any chance of Ginny being tracked down. That meant checking records of who had looked at public files, and removing them from following up. No witnesses. Guilt could be shifted to the missing person, and no one would suspect Cameron.

That was what finally kicked me out of the "Lone Rangerette" attitude. I'd potentially put Dean Youngwood in Cameron's crosshairs, because unlike me, he was a bit of a celebrity with the police, in a good way. He had to sign his name to look at Ginny's records at the precinct. It was pretty clear he had to have looked at them himself. He wouldn't have had all the detailed information he did without doing a thorough records search. That meant I had to do more research on Cameron myself — and Ginny, and her parents.

The question was: Did I have the time? The spell should last a while. But, if Cameron was a smart as he'd already shown, they might try to cast a spell to break any personal connections so methods like my tracking spell wouldn't work. So, I had an artificial time limit that had no real end point other than the nebulous words "real soon". I decided to swallow my pride and get some help.

I wished Fawn and Larry were available, but stomped on that idea immediately. I had to get others that were more used to this kind of off-the-cuff improvisation. Most importantly, Fawn had her unborn baby, and I didn't want that precious life to be in the line of fire.

"JC?" I looked up from the doodles that hadn't done much for inspiration. "You know anyone that you'd feel comfortable watching your back on this kind of job?"

JC opened up his guitar case, pulled out the old red-colored guitar, then tapped it closed with his foot. Somehow, I didn't flinch when the case was opened. He nestled the guitar between his thigh and arm, and made a show of tuning it.

"Hmmm, you're deciding that two isn't enough? I think that in this case, I agree with you. 'More is better.' Especially more in the form of a few tough customers." He strummed a few chords, then said, "You already got Dean Youngwood involved. He knows his way around a brawl. I worked around him once."

"I didn't realize you know Dean."

JC nodded.

"It took me a moment to realize you meant Youngwood. It was a while ago. He was tracking a ceremonial mask that'd been stolen from the Cree tribe. I was working for a private collector who wanted the mask for his collection. Let's say it wasn't the best way to make a first impression." He shrugged ruefully. "Dean beat me to it, and the fight wasn't much of one. He got the drop on me. I agreed to not getting shot, and letting him return the mask." JC chuckled at the memory.

"Beyond him, I can think of a few, but not really ones I'd want to rely on. They're good, just either a little too bloodthirsty, or more interested in what they can find to take home with them." He looked over to me and strummed another chord. "What about your contacts? A smart lady like yourself probably has a favor or two that could be called in?"

I thought about it. "There might be. How about we go look it over before I try to call in those favors? I'd rather know what we're looking at, so I can lay it out for our potential partners."

We both spun towards the office door as we heard the outer door open. The light came on in the small secretary office. I moved off to one side, kneeled behind my desk, and kept my eyes on the door.

JC flipped the guitar case open. I could hear faint wheezing coming from it. JC pulled a large caliber revolver out of his underarm holster and had it aimed at the door. A shadowy figure raised a hand and rapped on the frosted window.

"Ms. Fatelli? Are you here?" Sinera's throaty voice came to us as she fitted a key to the door.

"I'm here. Why are you here?"

Sinera opened the door as JC flipped the guitar case closed. He watched the Elf glide into the room, carrying a large, flat box. She was dressed in tight-fitting blue jeans and a brown leather coat. The sound of the coffee machine whirring to life, and the smell of it wafting in, reminded me I hadn't eaten for a while.

Sinera walked over to my desk, then leaned over to set the donuts on it. She straightened up, flipping her hair back with her left hand as she turned to face JC and I.

"I brought over some Tim Horton's donuts."

The warm yeasty smell rolled over to us as she opened the box. Eleven glazed donuts sat waiting. Sinera smiled, then plucked one from the box. "I had one earlier."

JC placed the guitar on top of its case, then walked over to grab two. He walked back, picked up the guitar, then used a toe to expertly flip the case open. He dropped both donuts into the case, which elicited a bone chilling series of chitters and yips. Sinera glanced at the case. Her eyes, like mine, widened at the sounds emanating from it. JC hooked his foot past the wide end of the case and closed it with a flick.

He put the guitar back on the case and took a big bite out of the remaining Tim Horton's specialty. He chewed a few times, then swallowed. He smiled and politely inclined his head towards Sinera.

"Thank you, ma'am. That was mighty thoughtful of you."

Sinera inclined her head at the compliment, then stepped back out of the room. She came back a moment later with a gallon of distilled water, and a half pound of coffee. She went to my large coffee urn, pulled out the filter, poured the entire contents of the coffee in, then added the gallon of water. She looked at both JC and I.

"You've a long night ahead of you. The coffee should help you maintain focus."

I couldn't argue with that.

# 15

AFTER AN HOUR OF STUDYING, random doodling while I tried to come up with ideas, and some random strumming from JC, Sinera stepped to the edge of my desk, then sat on the corner.

"I've a question for you, Ms. Fatelli."

"What's that?"

It wasn't unusual. Sinera had always been curious, and I've answered her questions about "trapping" as best as I could. Smart and competent help is hard to come by — and Sinera was both.

"Have you ever seen yourself as growing this business by taking a partner?"

The question sounded innocent and curious enough, but if you've spent time around the fae as I have, you learn that each question has depth to it, concealing one, or two, or more, questions entwined in the asking of one. This was one of those questions. I was guessing that Sinera was asking about me making her a partner.

She'd been totally absorbed in learning every detail about what I did and, in many instances, why I took the jobs I did, and rejected some others that were nearly identical.

It comes down to one question for me, and it's this one: In doing this job, have I stayed true to what I believe in? If I can answer "yes", then I'll do the job. If no, it's not one I should take.

It sounds kind of hypocritical to say it out loud, but it isn't. You have to have something you believe in. I believe in making choices that make things better in the long run. Short-term can hurt a lot, but the goal is what happens over time. I believe I can make a difference; I can make things better.

You could argue that I'm not baiting someone into infidelity, or presenting temptation, or like being hired to find records a person wants to disappear. That's business. It's the why behind things that's important.

Say, that the records I was supposed to find were of a person's involvement in drug smuggling, then that would be one I'd have to turn down. If the records I was tracking were being used for extortion — like, for example, as a way of putting pressure on a council member to vote city projects a certain way — then those records I have no compunction about stealing. Sure, it's all perspective — but it's my perspective, and how I choose to live.

I stared at Sinera as she awaited my answer.

"It depends on the prospective partner. For example, if a man or woman came to me as a prospective partner, and cared only about the pay, then they would be the wrong partner. If this person was a crusader and saw everything like a television detective? Well, the same answer. One is too invested in cash to consider morals first, and the other too consumed by them to look at consequences beyond the immediate."

I paused to study her reaction. She appeared to remain serene, as the elves do so well. But, after my experience with Cobb, I could read small tells that indicated she was thinking quite a bit about what she'd heard.

"If you found the right person, you'd consider taking on a partner or junior member."

I nodded. "That's what it renders down to: the right person, and the right perspective."

JC chuckled. "I think that's awful mighty and high thinking, Ms. Fatelli. How do you know the right person when you meet them? Unless you got the way to read their soul, you're taking anyone on a trial basis. And long-term? There ain't no way to predict long-term. You're no more likely to know if what you do is going have a beneficial effect, any more than you can say that the next person you meet is going to be a righteous, upright sort."

Sinera pushed off the desk, then faced me. "JC makes an interesting point. How can you decide a job on potential long-term benefits? That is unrealistic, and self-absorbed. I could hardly work for a person who thought so highly of themselves in such a manner."

The words grated. I didn't like the fact they didn't understand what I was after. To be truthful, maybe I did try to paint myself as a heroine going against the long odds and fighting the good fight. That old adage, "Everyone's a hero to themselves.", is very true. No one wants to be considered the bad guy … usually. Only people who get a kick with messing with the status quo see themselves as outlaws. Even they tend to see themselves as more a noble bandit than just a person out for themselves. I'd oversold myself … and gotten my face rubbed in it.

"Fine. Do what you want. I'm sure you have something you want, beyond looking for a partnership here. Right now," I motioned to JC, "We've got a kidnap victim that needs to be rescued. So if that is all that's on your mind, then it can wait until after we get Ginny back from Cameron."

Sinera nodded. "I will not interrupt your planning. You are welcome for the Tim Horton's."

JC frowned at me, then lifted his eyes towards Sinera's retreating back.

"What? You have something to say?"

All this silent judgment was really getting to me. I was suddenly sick and tired of the whole thing. It could have been stress — the loss of Zhirk, Kevin, and Kent — but suddenly partners was the absolute worst idea in the world. I got lost in my own head. Not in a good way.

JC, Sinera … who needed them? They'd just get in the way and get hurt when fertilizer hit the rotating blades. Who was I kidding? I'd brought it on myself. This was crazy. How could I do anything about Ginny — and Cameron — without screwing up more than I already had. Talking big … Yeah, like that's gonna help someone. It was then that JC slapped me across the face.

The crack of his hand spun me, and the chair I was sitting in, halfway around to face the windows. While I was dazed, JC clamped down on my wrists and held me in the chair.

"Ms. Fatelli, whatever you're doing, you need to stop. I'm not an Orc that likes to strike a female, but you are certainly acting nothing like yourself the last few minutes. How about you sit there and I'll call Ms. Sinera back."

It wasn't a question. I thought about struggling, but couldn't move as images flashed in my mind. I just sat there, seeing Zhirk, Kevin, and Kent. It barely registered that my hands were shaking after JC released them. I couldn't breathe. My heart started hammering. Panic squeezed my chest. My vision started to grey out.

And then the dam broke.

I started crying. I think I screamed a lot. My throat was hoarse and sore when JC picked me up. I don't remember falling out of the chair. All I remember is JC picking me up and holding me while Sinera lowered the Murphy bed. After pulling the bed down, Sinera followed JC to the door, turning off the light before she pulled the door closed behind her. The door muffled their voices as they talked about something I couldn't quite hear. It wouldn't have mattered anyway, I was so lost in the pent-up grief and guilt. I just sobbed into my pillow, and tried to shut out the sounds.

I fell asleep finally, but my dreams were of Kevin's screams as Cobb tortured him to death, and Kent's bleak face when Cobb dragged him away. It repeated again and again as I screamed in silence. The last image I remember seeing before I fell into darkness was watching Zhirk dying as half his face was blasted away by the Nephilim, Ahiah.

# 16

I AWOKE IN SWEAT-DRENCHED, CLAMMY PANTS AND SHIRT. To my dubious credit, I didn't scream. I just sat upright in the bed until my heart slowed down enough that it didn't feel like I was choking on it. I wanted to stay in bed, shut out the day, and forget everything I was supposed to do. My conscience wouldn't let me. That annoying little voice yammered at me until I finally started moving.

The brightness of the light through the open curtains made it easy to find my shoes without tripping over them. I pushed the Murphy bed up and opened the top drawer of the gold-colored file cabinet on the left, getting out a pair of socks, bra, a pair of blue jeans from the second drawer, and an old red April Wine t-shirt. The previously worn clothes went in the bottom drawer with the other dirty clothes to be washed at the nearby laundromat.

I needed to get moving. Ginny was in real trouble, and I needed to move. I strode to the door … and I … couldn't. I couldn't reach for the doorknob. I wanted to walk down to the local 'Y' to get a shower. I needed to rescue Ginny. My hand refused to move towards the doorknob. If I could have just willed myself to move, I'd already be on the road. I vaguely noticed that my hands were shaking. My body joined my hands, shaking so badly I nearly collapsed. My heart joined in, racing my body to see which happened first: collapse or heart attack.

I staggered, whimpering, back to the Murphy bed and collapsed onto it. My mouth felt gritty and foul. I hadn't brushed my teeth; my breath was stale and stank like rotted food. My armpits smelled awful. I wanted a shower, but I just couldn't leave the room. It was out there — everything that hurt.

I couldn't get myself to face it. I thought maybe after some more rest I could. I pulled the covers over my head, tears starting to leak from my eyes.

I curled tighter under the covers, heart racing, with hoarse sobs coming from me. If you've ever had a panic attack, you know just how bad it hits, how much you get screwed up emotionally. I didn't, and couldn't understand why I felt so helpless. That desolate feeling of powerlessness beat down on me. It was a feedback spiral. I couldn't, so I didn't, and hated myself, and couldn't, so I didn't, *et cetera, et cetera*. On and on in the same loop in my head.

The doorknob turned, the sound of which hit my ears like a gunshot. I screamed and curled tighter. Strong hands pulled the covers away, then drew me into a hug. Fawn. I knew it was Fawn.

I grabbed her and buried my face against her stomach and cried. Fawn sat on the bed and held me until my sobbing slowed down. Sinera had also entered at some point. She stood next to

Fawn, waiting patiently while holding a tray with fresh coffee and a brown paper bag.

"You need to eat. You've had a hard night, and you look like death warmed over."

That's Sinera. Wonderful bedside manner. She sat the tray on the edge of my desk. Turning to leave, she stopped and looked back over her shoulder.

"I went with Mr. JC last night. The location on the map is a compound, with barbed wire fences and gun towers. You should see it for yourself."

I nodded, still terrified and staring at the open mouth of the door, which I fully expected to sprout teeth and gnash Sinera to paste. She walked out, pulling the door closed after her.

Once it had shut, the pressure on my chest eased. I could breathe again. As my heart slowed, and the panicky sensations eased, my stomach chose that moment to remind me that I'd not eaten.

The smell from the bag was delicious, and set my mouth to watering. I looked up at Fawn, who opened her arms. Slowly standing up, I walked timidly to the desk, and opened the bag to see a lump wrapped in foil. Opening the foil revealed three pancakes wrapped around sausage - pigs in blankets. I tore into them, eating quickly, then followed a swallow with coffee.

As the warmth of the food and coffee hit my stomach, a slow spread of relaxation went through me, easing clenched jaw muscles, calming my mind. Fawn smiled tentatively, and I was surprised at the stretching of my cheek muscles making a smile in return.

The room returned to being a room; the door was just a door. I didn't have the panic: the overwhelming dread that had been my constant companion. Now I was cleaner, both physically and mentally, like the meal had sluiced away a lot of the psychological dirt that had covered my mind. I was able to function again. All the calm had me thinking about Fawn.

She was here, obviously. I looked out the window to the right of the desk, just in case I was dreaming. The warmth of the food and coffee suffused me with well-being. I saw my sister's black Lexus in the parking lot. The car was part of the RCMP motor pool, assigned to her for work — which sure beat my battered PT Cruiser that she'd parked next to.

The Lexus' sleek gloss black made it look like a big cat, poised for action. Next to it, the PT Cruiser resembled a weather-beaten black mushroom. The sight actually made me smile. There was something in the back of my head, though, as I thought of how funny the two cars were, a faint whispering that wouldn't quit. Part of my head sloshed and pulsed, like a sinus had been plugged. A little pressure, noticeable if I paid attention, but not painful or irritating. Just ... there.

I opened the office door to see Sinera at the large reception desk. She nodded, proffering a hot cider as I stood in the doorway.

"Have a cider. You look less ... incapacitated than a little bit ago. You must be feeling better."

The cider really hit the spot as I took a long drink, savoring the apple and spices on my tongue. The taste and aroma was so soothing that the voices and the pressure just faded, swallowed by the textures of the spice. It was like sinking into a warm bath.

Fawn stood up and walked over to me from the Murphy bed. Her blue eyes locked on mine as her gaze searched me for something. I stared right back.

Fawn broke eye contact first.

She fidgeted as she spoke. "Fern, I think I'm going to need your help. There's been a kidnapping, and ..." She struggled with finding the right words. "Because there's missing students from the Haven Academy."

She stared down at me from over fifty centimeters higher than my roughly one and one-half meter height. I was surprised that she'd come to me about something. Up to this point in my professional life, it'd been the other way around. I got some information from her, and shared when it was the proper thing to do. This was the first time she'd come to me.

"I looked at this from every angle, hoping to use the law, but the law's tied. It can't do anything unless a crime's reported, and those involved haven't done so."

She started pacing. Over to the file cabinets, then to the wall, along the wall to a point near the desk, then she turned to the desk and walked up to it, gazed at me while talking, then started over on the path.

"The girls are missing, and their parents say they're not. The Haven school said she ran off with another student. Then we're told that the report was placed by an overwrought instructor. My cop sense says 'bull'. There's got to be something. The school is wanting to press for an investigation, but the parents are refusing to cooperate."

Fawn turned and paced back in the opposite direction. "We've gone to the school, but for some reason they're refusing to go against the parents' wishes. They're withholding evidence, and that's a crime. But, because of the law, a kidnapping cannot be declared unless the child is reported missing. I can arrest the parents and the school staff on suspicion, but with the power and influence the Camerons have, and the prestige of the school, I'd be a bleeding body in shark-infested water."

She finished another circuit. Her head was bowed and she rubbed the back of her neck with a hand constantly.

"None of the students or teachers I've talked to have had anything useful to say about Ginny Cameron or this Pyrrha Holdwell."

Something in me wanted to cringe a little when Fawn mentioned my alias at the school, but the cider was so soothing I just sat, content to just sip as Fawn paced. I took another sip of the cider, feeling the soothing warmth spread through me. Sinera knew how to whip up cider.

The spicy apple aroma floated me to a soft place that had me sensing all of Fawn's frustration with her perceived helplessness. I could do something about that. I knew all the ins and outs of what happened at the school. I started to consider telling her the whole truth about what was going on.

Oh, to be sure, there was a frightened and cynical part of me, even through the soft glow of the cider, that kept me from speaking immediately. Why did I want to hide what could help my sister? I knew I was involved, but staying silent was really eating at me. Fawn picked up on my mood, like only a sister can.

"What's with you, Fern?"

She only called me Fern when she was worried about me.

She waited for me to answer, but I was suddenly struggling with whispering voices, pressure behind my eyes, and the soothing feelings of the cider. It was starting to twist things around. There had to be a way to change my path in all of this confusion. My instincts were to keep quiet, just as the voices whispered louder, and the whispered gibbering drew at me, trying to pull me into some kind of horrid nightmare that hovered at the edge of the cider. I drank some more — gulped it, actually — and the whispers receded, along with the pressure.

Fawn was looking at me with real concern now.

"Fern, talk to me. What's happening? Fern? Fern!?" She began to reach for me.

I froze between heartbeats, the icy shackles of fear locking my mind in terror. Fawn saw the panic and pulled me into a hug. The cider's soothing warmth shriveled, and then broke like a pane of glass. Horror crawled through the dark and burst forth, gibbering madly at the inside of my head, making it reverberate like an overfilled echo chamber.

The giggling, tittering shrieks of JC's abomination rolled spiked pain through my ears as Kevin Love's agonized screams bounced sharply off the inner walls of my skull. Kent Nix's groans were claws that tore at the back of my eyes, and the shotgun blast scattered images of Zhirk toppling throughout my vision. I wailed — a lost soul surrounded by hungry oblivion.

Fawn grabbed me in a desperate hug, holding me tight as I screamed and cried my heart out. The soft aroma of the soothing cider had worked loose the anchors that guilt had set in my soul. I cried as I purged the pain and loss for I don't know how long. My sister held me through it all. When I finally started to settle down, the grief was still there.

It was sharp, painful, but the pain was a healing scab — not the overwhelming wound in the heart that I'd saddled myself with. I had nearly drowned in it, and now I was finally getting my head back above water for the first time in a long while.

I looked up at Fawn through what I was sure was red-rimmed eyes and with a snotty nose. I wanted to say something smart and witty to hold the intimacy away, but all I could say was … nothing. Words couldn't convey the mix of emotions in my chest.

Fawn tightened her embrace, holding me for a long moment.

"I've seen that in a few cops. Especially new ones getting caught in a life-or-death moment. I can't stop it from messing you up, sis. But I'm here when you want me."

Her words started me crying again. We sat together for a while longer. As the terror receded to regret, my internal censor was still whispering not to let Fawn know about the school or Ginny. It wasn't nearly as strident, sounding now more like a tired watchman too old to really care. I hadn't talked to JC or

Sinera at all. I knew there was a compound, but that was all I knew.

Compounds meant usually a large group that wanted to be away from prying eyes for many sorts of reasons. What that might be could be a cult, or a group of fae trying to keep themselves untainted by humanity, or a leper colony.

Yes, leprosy is still around, and was one of the first diseases that incorporated magick into it. It's slow, incurable, and inevitably lethal if you're unlucky enough to catch it. Thankfully, it's very hard to catch. I doubted it was a leper colony. Those are very open about where they are so that afflicted can find them, give them comfort, and a place to belong.

I went for the more likely: either a cult, or a militia. Either choice meant very narrow-minded individuals, usually carrying weapons to back up their arguments with violence. Going in guerrilla-style to rescue Ginny was likely to be very dangerous and, if it was a militia, that meant more guns and, in some cases, actual combat training, which also upped the danger.

Militias didn't typically go after women. The best guess was a cult of some kind. That made a rotten sort of sense. The David Cameron we'd met was a pastor. How hard would it be for a pastor to whip people up with religious fervor?

In either case, going in alone, or in a small group, could work. But any slip-up, and no one would get out. Getting a whole horde of police and RCMP MaRS and TAC units would be a lot more comforting. It carried risk, as any group that big would not do well with stealth.

Despite what you might see on TV, stealth isn't typical of a TAC or MaRS unit. They're deployed for special conditions. It becomes a chess match: what defenses the perpetrator had versus RCMP training and tactics.

I turned the thought over in my head and came to the conclusion that Fawn needed to know. I could hedge the story some. I didn't like that, but it would keep me from getting crosswise to her as a cop.

Maybe that was it: Talk to her as a private citizen. It was kind of a moral stretch to ask her just to be a civilian that I talked to, but I could only ask. Fawn was straight-up direct. If she could do it, she'd tell you; if she couldn't, she'd tell you.

My mental shoulder angel said to hang the indecision and ask, rather than letting the other shoulder guy work me up.

# 17

I HAD TO MAKE A DECISION and get off the fence.

"Uh, Fawn. Can I talk with you about something? I need my sister to talk with me, not 'My Sister, The Cop'. Could you do that for me?"

I think Fawn wrestled with it for a few moments. She got very still, and her eyes got a distant look to them.

"It'd be hard, Fern. I really don't like it, but if you want it to be off the record, I'll listen."

"Off the record" meaning, "My Sister, The Cop". But it was better than not talking at all.

"Okay, this is edited. But it's something you should know. I was going to tell you about it after what else was going on got cleared up."

So instead of talking about Ginny, I told her about Mrs. Villers and the MC, laying out what JC and I had found going on and our suspicions.

Fawn's mouth set in a thin line as I got to the end of the edited narrative. Fawn stood up. She was in full cop mode then.

"So you got this by investigating the school." She opened her mouth, then shut it and shook her head. "What you've described is something that needs to be taken care of right now. I can call you as a witness. Whatever's going on doesn't have to be part of the investigation."

I thought for a moment. "Maybe, Fawn, you could just say you heard rumors about security at the school, and that to prove or deny the security problems, you hired a private investigator do a surveillance check, which exposed the mind-magick. Would that work for a dodge?"

I think Fawn warmed to the idea, as the RCMP on occasion did hire people to test security. But those were usually high-security sites. A school wouldn't typically be on that kind of list, except that darn near all the one-percenters sent their kids to Haven. It had that big a reputation as a school that turned out top students for college — and nearly all had gone on to manage family fortunes, businesses, or both.

You don't get that kind of recognition without some serious chops to back it up. So, while unusual, the prestige, money, and political power centered in one place could be a good reason for a RCMP official to hire a private investigator to check the security over, rather than sending a cop to do the job. In or out of uniform, cops just have that "cop" aura. If you've family or close friends in law enforcement, you probably have seen or sensed it for yourself. Unless they are great actors, it's there.

I am so not cop. It would fly, so long as nothing else stirred the pot. I could get on with the rescue of the kidnapped Ginny, and thereby save my business reputation — and my own peace of mind. I still was reluctant to tell Fawn, though. My pride was risking Ginny's life by keeping Fawn out of the loop. There was no doubt Fawn could help, but would it be enough and, more importantly, what would it do to our relationship?

I was so wrapped in what it meant to me, I nearly missed what would it do to Larry and Fawn. I sat down at my desk as she paced, thinking about what I'd said to her.

I was the older than Fawn by about a minute. We're obviously not identical twins, but we are, at least to my thinking, very close. Fawn is a comic-book Amazon brought to life, with blonde hair, piercing blue eyes, with a body close to two meters in height that carried ninety kilograms of feminine curves and hard muscle. She earned her post: Valedictorian in school, top athlete. She was THE girl in every grade.

When we turned eighteen, I moved out of Uncle Todd and Aunt Ruthie's house as fast as I could. I, being slightly over one and one-half meters tall, and maybe forty kilograms, with fire-red hair, was pretty much the rebel growing up. The small kid, big chip-on–the-shoulder type. Despite these stark differences, we were sisters, and that meant the world to both of us.

I failed the RCMP entrance test, drifted a year through numerous minimum wage jobs, and finally got myself together when I was twenty. I passed the examination for a private investigator license a year later. Fawn blew the RCMP exam out of the water at the same time I failed, scoring the highest marks in the class. She became a cop at nineteen, continued her education in college, and graduated with a law degree. All the while doing beat cop work.

Beat cop? You heard right. She walked the streets in full uniform. With her figure, she got a lot of attention, and her natural charm made it easy for her to connect to the neighborhoods she patrolled. But you heard right: a beat cop.

Someone in Halifax politics came up with the idea that more police, and more visibility, would help deter crime — and especially deter hate crimes. So instead of investing in a lot of cars, they invested more in people. And by people, I mean every race that wanted to join was allowed to join, if they could pass the physical and legal tests.

I was caught between two choices: Fawn's involvement, and Ginny's life. Weighed that way, there wasn't a choice. I hated it. Ginny. What am I going to do about her? If I hide what's going on, my sister will be …

I shook my head. Fawn stopped her pacing as she reached the desk, then looked down towards me, concern in her eyes.

"Fern? You look scared."

Look? Hell, I *was* scared. I didn't want to lose Fawn's trust, and I didn't want Ginny to get hurt. It was time to come clean.

Selfish? Maybe. Maybe I had too much guilt still in me from losing friends. I didn't know how to answer myself, so all I could do was go with what my beliefs said was right. I had to decide.

I got off the fence and, with a lot of guilt, spilled everything to Fawn. I think I saw a glint of approval in Sinera's eyes. The Elf stood just inside the closed office door. I know she had been outside. How she got into the room and closed a squeaky office door without making any noise is a trick I'd like to learn.

Fawn's cop face got stiffer as she listened. I had a hard time looking up at her from my desk chair. She started pacing again, this time faster, and lots more agitated.

"Geez, Shorty, I can't just let it go. You know that. Kidnapping is a felony, no matter what the reason."

I nodded. I looked down at my hands. I didn't want to look at Fawn. I knew she had to choose and, that choosing either way, she was going to lose something. If she chose the law, she'd have to arrest me and charge me with kidnapping. If she chose not to, then she was ignoring the whole reason she became a cop: to keep people safe and uphold the law. Justice was in there too and, while she may think what I did was just, it wasn't by any stretch of imagination legal.

As she paced back towards the desk, I raised my head.

"Fawn, how about a compromise? Help me get Ginny back and we can sort this out when she's safe. I'll go along with anything you say."

It was a big shift from protecting my reputation. I know that a reputation is how a person in my line of work is judged. That's important to me. It's how I get clients. Discretion and success are what you're measured by. It was the same for Fawn. A good cop counts for a lot versus just an okay cop.

"I can go with that. And we'll have a sit down after we get Ginny away from that slimeball. Deal?"

"Deal," I agreed.

It was also rather telling that neither of us talked about what might happen if we were caught. I don't think Fawn wanted to think about what that meant for her baby. I know I didn't want to think about that at all. Her and the baby dying was THE terror that would be with me until this was all over.

Fawn sighed as if a weight lifted from her shoulders. She straightened, then twisted her head left and right to loosen it. The sound of her muscles cracking was a testimonial to how tightly wound she'd been.

"I do this one off the books. I'm included in everything. I've got a lot of vacation time and sick days coming to me, so I can spend some on this. I'll call in to schedule the sick day."

Fawn strode purposely to the outer office and called her station. She informed them she was needed to take some "personal time". I heard her say "yes" a few times, along with more talking. Then she hung up, clapping her folding cell phone shut, and walked back into the inner office.

JC sauntered in, following Fawn. "Well, it looks like your little drink and talk had some benefits, don'tcha think?" His deep baritone held a chuckle as he finished speaking.

Sinera nodded to the big Orc. "It has had some unexpected results. An effective purge, for now."

She looked to Fawn, who returned her gaze with her eyebrows raised in an unspoken question. JC chuckled again and the two women's gazes turned towards him.

He raised his hands up in mock surrender. "Ladies, please. How about we figure out how we're going to get at the matter at hand? That little girl's out there with who knows what going on around her. I think we need to settle that mess before we decide to settle anything else."

# 18

I T TOOK MOST OF AN HOUR to get to talk with Dean. He surprised me by agreeing immediately.

"It's all good to me. You got that girl out of a rough home, and some fast-talker kidnapped her from you. You got set up and, by extension, me. I don't like being used that way, even indirectly. Count me in."

That made it four.

"I'm going too."

Sinera's voice was firm. The mulish part of me wanted to say no, but she obviously wasn't going to listen — and JC had already taken her out to the site. He obviously thought she could handle herself. I didn't have a reason to really say no.

"Okay, you're in."

Fawn already had included herself. Now, she had to talk to Larry and tell him what was going on. I cringed mentally, imagining what he would be like when he found out that his wife — and unborn child — were going into a compound full of hostile, and likely armed, people. She left to talk with him alone, face to face. I'm glad she didn't ask me to go. Larry would chew me up and spit me out for this.

I was still convinced she shouldn't be along, but there was no way she'd let us go without her. Larry couldn't go. He didn't have any training. He didn't know combat magick. He refused to use a weapon of any kind. He'd be toast the moment things went sideways.

I went to the battered gold file drawer and opened it, then moved all my authentic breakables off the desk into some towels and stored them in the top drawer. What was left was my green-tinted banker's lamp, some pens and pencils, and a lot of bare, open space on the desk for pictures, maps, and notebooks.

We waited for two hours for Fawn to get back. She was pale and silent as she walked back through the door. I knew without asking that it had been bad. Fawn looked like she'd been stabbed in the heart. All I could do was give her a quick hug and maneuvered her to the Murphy bed to sit down.

JC took one of the armless guest chairs in front of the desk, then turned it around and sat down, chest against the back. The chair creaked ominously under his weight. He leaned into the back of the chair and rested his arms on top. He gave me a smile, and rakish two-finger salute.

"Ready for orders, ma'am."

Fawn looked over to me, and made herself take part. "I think, Sis, we need to wait for this Dean guy you called. If we don't, we'll just be doing a recap when he gets here."

It sounded good to me. The stress of confessing to Fawn, and the stress of seeing how hard talking to Larry was on her, made me stressed. Which made me hungry.

Me, the practical girl I am, called Papa Torino's for a pizza delivery. Pizza's a staple when you're living without a kitchen in your place. Just like the 'Y' is a substitute shower room. The four pizzas arrived at the same time as Dean, so eating and planning ended up going hand in hand.

Between bites of supreme toppings, Dean filled the others in on Ginny's background. Then I explained about all the ruckus at Haven, describing how Ginny and I made our impromptu escape from the school, and, even though we didn't need it for this, I added in how Mrs. Villers controlled the Haven school with mind-magick. Recapping done, it was time for JC and Sinera to explain what they saw at the compound. JC started first.

"It's kind of in a long six-sided place. The long side's around three hundred meters, and the short sides are angled, and about a hundred meters. It looks kind of like an angular canoe with both ends being pointed. Each end has a deer stand: one of those canvas and wood platforms, or small tree house, that hunters use to hide in trees, which is a guard post. The flaps were drawn down on the windows all the time, so neither of us got a look inside it."

He sketched out the compound. To me it looked like a stub of a pencil sharpened at both ends. He drew seven X's on the picture: one at the angles of the east and west ends, one in the middle of the north side, then two on the south side close together. The end points on the east and west had no towers. Sinera took up the narrative from there.

"These two deer stands are on the gate. The fence is eight-foot tall hurricane, with barbed wire in loops at the top. It will be difficult to get through or over quickly. The fence has black plastic sheets zip-tied to the fence, which obscured the compound from ground level. Fortunately, they only cleared the trees about twelve meters back from the fence, and there are a number of large pines tall enough to see over the fence and into the compound."

She nodded to JC, who nodded and motioned her to continue. She was silent for a moment, then continued.

"The compound inside is made of a series of square and rectangular buildings. The rectangular ones were nearly dark, with a small amount of light shining through shutters. The two largest buildings were completely blacked out, and had guards posted by them.

"It is my supposition that those buildings are where prisoners are kept. Some of the other buildings were open and lit. One on each side of the camp was especially busy, so likely they are barracks, or additional security posts."

Sinera stopped to let us think about the information, then JC picked up the narrative.

"Those deer stands had teams of two relieve the original watchers. So the estimate is two men per tower. Sinera counted four guarding the prison buildings, and another eight more patrolling the inside of the compound. If we guess three shifts of guards to be conservative, that would make potentially sixty-six.

"They were all male, and not all human. Sinera saw Hamref, Troykin, and a Troll during our observation. The compound does not appear to have enough buildings to hold that many guards. The best estimate, based on what Sinera and I observed, is around forty."

He paused once more to let the information sink in. I think my heart lurched to hear about the Troll. Zhirk would have been disappointed to know that a Troll was helping kidnap a girl.

Sinera gazed at all of us as she said, "I believe they are expecting us to show. They were all alert, and suspicious of any sound." She looked at the rest of us, then back down to the table. "I do not know if the weapons are correct, but most appeared to be shotguns and hunting rifles. There were some black, military-styled weapons also."

That got our attention. Despite the government ban, it was easy to get kits to convert a semi-automatic to full. If they had been converted, that would be a dangerous increase in firepower. Like I said, the conversion is illegal. But if you're a cultist, why care about the law? It's all about having the power to enforce your will on others.

My snubnose was technically restricted under the old gun control laws of Canada. As an heirloom, it went back in the family to the 1940's, when my great-something grandfather, who was an American peace officer, used it as a second weapon rigged up on his boot. Since I was oldest, I got the pistol, which still is in pristine shape after magick came back. Someone had it cleaned up. It had parts that were replaced and artificially aged, so the story goes.

The laws are different now. Weapons are pretty much everywhere, as you're never certain where some big, ugly, and carnivorous thing will jump out of a shadow, intent on eating you. Fawn's MaRS team uses a ten-millimeter rifles and twelve-gauge semi-automatic shotguns for standard gear.

We had a good idea what we were up against. We knew roughly how many, an idea what they had for weapons, and the layout, with a reasonable guess where Ginny might be kept. The obvious question was: were we sure of any of this? No. There was no way to tell without days of proper surveillance and, if they were even the tiniest bit aggressive at searching outside the compound, a recon team could be spotted.

I wanted to put it off, but in my mind I didn't think we could. If they wanted Ginny so badly, there had to be a reason. Using me to get her meant that they wanted the reason hidden. I just wish I understood why. If we knew why they wanted her, that might influence how they kept her, and where. It might even affect how we approached this situation. Little voices in my mind urged me to go, right now, and others whispered that I needed to hide. I shook my head, and the noise faded a bit.

"Hey, Sinera? When you were looking in the camp, was there anything like decorations up or pictures?"

She stood absolutely still for a moment, then replied quietly, "There were some, regularly placed on each building above the doors that I could see the front of. It was a long pole with a curve at the end."

Fawn's eyes lit up. "I know that one. The Shepherds. They're a pretty fringe group. It's too bad too, because they don't care about what you are, just what you believe in. If you don't believe in the Reverend, or the Reverend's words, you're one of the Godless." She paused to think for a moment. "RCMP has them on a watch list. They're suspected of promoting violence. Two churches near Lake Echo were destroyed by arson. Both cases are going cold for lack of evidence."

JC nodded as Fawn finished. "They sound like a rough bunch to get crosswise of."

Fawn nodded. "That was the opinion of the RCMP also. There are some recorded altercations, but nothing major enough to search their church. Proving that Ginny is being held against her will at the Shepherd compound will give us a reason to present an 'Information to Obtain' and get a warrant. Does that tracker you made still work? That would seal the deal."

I went and got the uniform in its plastic bag, then fed power into the spell. The spell activated, but the bag didn't tug at me. I put the bag down. The little yammering voices raised in pitch, but not strong enough that I had trouble controlling myself.

"No. Someone erased Ginny's signature, or put her in a protective ward. It's just a torn-up school uniform now."

Fawn grimaced. "Just once it'd be nice to have something easy."

JC chuckled. Sinera frowned and went to mix up a glass of cider, while Dean looked at the drawing of the compound.

"How much time do you think we have to scout this out before going in?" He rubbed his cheek with his left hand while pulling a cigar tube from his back pocket.

"Uh uh, not in here, Dean. Take that smoke stick outside if you're going to light up." Dean looked at me with a sheepish grin, then slid the cigar back into its tube, which went back into his back pocket.

"I know, it's a stinky habit, but it helps me think when I'm stuck on something."

That statement piqued my curiosity. "What are you stuck on?"

He shrugged and gestured at the drawing of the compound. "That thing. You're on uneven ground, and they had to cut a clearing from thick bunch of trees. Why go through the trouble to make the compound so long when it'd be easier to defend if it was more square or round? Why angle the ends? I don't get why it's got all the buildings in the center, with all that open ground at the angled sections. You don't need a practice ground that big, and something three football fields long, and less than one wide, is an awful skinny thing to me." He tapped his finger on the map. "The buildings here at the center are so crowded together makes it a little easier to guard, but a lot easier to sneak from building to building. Prisoners should be out in some isolated spot, with extra wire and a tower or two, to my thinking."

He took a breath and released it slowly. "You all can laugh if you want, but my gut's saying that there's a reason for the structure being built like that. A reason we won't like."

We'd all stopped to listen. Dean, like all of us, had gone through some hard knocks growing up, and his profession — pardon, *our* profession — relied on gut instinct to recognize trouble. According to Dean, who might have familiarity with something like this, this place is unusual. He sensed it, and trusted his feeling. My gut feeling was drowned out by the voices telling me to give up and just huddle in a corner.

"Well, I am more intrigued than ever about this little place," JC said with a smile. "Seems like a right interesting conundrum we're mixed up in."

Dean and Sinera nodded in unison.

Fawn sighed, the moved on to the next topic. "I think we should determine what we need for this situation, and begin discussing how we enter the compound."

Sinera handed me the cup of cider. I took it gratefully, and enjoyed a sip. The warmth, and the soothing flavor, rolled down my throat, spreading a sense of comfort and serenity. The faint voices in my head faded entirely as the warmth spread through me.

"So we're going to go for sneak in/sneak out, or blow the doors down?"

I couldn't help it. I giggled. I was so totally mellow everything was funny.

Fawn looked over at Sinera, who was looking intently at me. "What did you do to that cider?"

Sinera turned her head towards Fawn.

"I did nothing to the cider. I spelled the cup."

Dean looked up, alarmed at the drunk-sounding giggles coming from me. As Sinera walked towards me, I chugged the cider and sat bonelessly in my chair, turning into a warm, cozy puddle of human. I oozed from the chair onto the floor, still giggling like a happy drunk. JC picked me up, and cradled me in one burly arm as he delicately carried me to the Murphy bed and placed me on it.

I don't remember anything else after that.

# 19

I WOKE THE NEXT MORNING feeling better than I had in a while. The day was bright and cloudless, with the sun still a brilliant orange. It was the last bit of fall before the storms of winter.

After I'd finished my shower at the 'Y', I started to turn over Dean's words again in my mind: Why the odd shape? It didn't look odd to me, but then I'd never been around a "normal" compound — or any kind of one for that matter. Fawn's words about them being religious fanatics had gotten my attention. That didn't sound like there'd be any room for talk, so I gave up on the idea of talking Cameron into letting Ginny go.

The sidewalk guided me back to my office, where Sinera had shown up in uncharacteristic blue jeans and a forest-green shirt. Her hair was wrapped in a bun with two sticks holding her hair in place, making her Elven, pointed ears stand out dramatically.

I'd never seen Sinera dress so casually before. Her slender neck looked even thinner without her hair hanging down. She held out a cup of coffee towards me as I entered the outer office.

"No thanks, I'm feeling pretty awake."

Sinera shrugged and set it on her desk, then began to look through the equipment that had been collected while I was at the 'Y'. There were some coils of rope and web belts to hold gear. Sinera was ordering online. I left her to go back into my office and find out what I'd missed. I'd passed out before anything was decided, so I wanted to harass JC about it. The Orc was in one of the guest chairs in front of my desk. He'd gotten back to the office sometime while I was at the 'Y'. He had the guitar in his lap, polishing its surface with a soft-looking white cloth. When that "Shambler" giggled and hissed, he tapped his foot against the guitar case. I wondered if it was restless, or knew about the things we were planning to do later. JC was going to bring it, I knew, and we'd likely be grateful for its help, but it was one thing I hoped I'd never have to experience again.

My stomach chose that moment to remind me that I hadn't eaten since last night. It was close to noon and, since I didn't have a refrigerator, it was time to go find a meal. JC said he'd be back later in the afternoon. Sinera volunteered to go tag along, after she asked me to pick up a quick meal for her. The closest place was a small diner a few blocks away.

So, after JC and Sinera left, I went over to Francis' Diner and got two plates of eggs, sausage, and a waffle to go. When I returned, I left Sinera's plate on her desk. Then I went back into the inner office, and got to paying bills. After finishing the bills, and my meal, I pulled down the Murphy bed at noon and crawled in. I wanted to be rested for tonight. I've never gone courting trouble like this. Single encounters, sure. Walking into an armed camp of gun-toting crazies? No. Not something on my bucket list.

I didn't want to do this. It was totally out of my depth. I was scared that this was going to be a big mistake … that I was going to die. I tossed and turned, trying to quiet the little harbinger of doom that kept whispering in my ear, then gave it up and threw the sheets back.

I rolled out of the bed, dressed in black skin-tight leggings and pullover, then put on the web belt JC said I ought to get. The holster clipped on easily, and I hooked on three pouches: one carrying extra ammo speed-loaders for the .357 magnum snubnose revolver, a second pouch with a first aid kit, and a third with zip strips, candy, and a mirror.

After debating it, I put on a fourth pouch holding twenty-gauge shotgun shells for the "Howdah" twenty-gauge pistol grip sawed-off shotgun. The shotgun was loaded with Number One buckshot, as that held more pellets, and would hurt just about anything. If the Troll came my way, I was running. I didn't want to face a raging Troll. That would be too painful, and too much for me to handle alone — and probably too much to handle even with help.

I had a head mount for a small flashlight, and two sheaths for Sykes-Fairburn daggers. Holy Rambo, I was an Action Heroine off to go save the day with overwhelming violence.

I hate violence. It's the first resort of the crazy and/or desperate — and the last resort of the smart ones.

The boots I got were the steel-toe variety, along with hard knee pads, elbow pads, and a face mask to accessorize the ensemble. I wanted my body protected, and the steel toes would be a nasty extra bit of *oomph* if I had, gods forbid, to go hand to hand with one of the fanatics.

I grabbed a coffee cup off my desk. The cup was full and steaming warm. Heaven. I took a couple hefty gulps, then, after setting the coffee cup back on the desk, I laid down on the bed, ready to go, waiting for the others. Somewhere in all those tense moments, I passed out. Sinera and her spelled cups, again. *Stupid Elf magick …*

The next thing I remember was being gently shaken awake by Sinera. She had dressed like me, *sans* face mask. The others were also there. JC and Fawn were elected as team leaders, with Fawn in overall charge. She had the most experience, and had been the one to steer us towards the supply stores for uniforms and things. It was also she who said I ought to go with the double-barreled hand cannon, saying that, since I'd never fired a rifle, it would be a good substitute. All the others, excepting Sinera, were loaded up with FN-FAL 7.62 rifles, and large ten-millimeter pistols.

I was to go with Sinera, who was armed with a loop of leather that held more knives than I cared to think about. They were all slim, triangular, and razor-sharp on their edges, with deep grooves. I don't know if it was hubris on her part, or if she was actually that good. Fawn cradled the FN-FAL like it was part of her. She looked every bit the Amazon. She split us in teams of two: Dean and JC, Sinera and myself. Fawn would jump between the two teams as we moved through the compound, and keep us on track.

The final part of the plan was to use one of the towers to get in. Sinera was a magick caster and, supposedly, according to her, decent to good at spells. She had a particular invisibility spell that was a lot like my "Don't notice me" one. We wouldn't be truly invisible; we'd just look like a natural part of whatever we were close to — like looking like a shrub if we were standing near one.

Sinera said slow movements were good, fast were bad, because the spell couldn't keep up with rapid movement. There'd be a flicker as the spell tried to compensate. Slow would get us into a tower, from where we could scan the grounds before going in. It was the best plan for the situation. We'd find out how good of one when we began.

There's an old truism that says, "The best developed plan never survives first contact with the enemy." No one acts like expected, so don't expect them to. You need to have a clear goal, and be able to react to the situation, changing as it changes. Yeah. Easy to say, hard to do. I've already had that little experience back at Haven.

Before we left my office, Fawn had made all of us write letters. It was kind of creepy. I hadn't thought of it, but the letters were there as evidence in case the worst happened and we didn't come home. Other officers could look at the letters and go from there. I wanted to burn mine as soon as I got back home, which I think is partly why Fawn had us do it. I wonder what Fawn wrote in hers to Larry ... how would she attempt to justify risking herself and her unborn baby in this kind of operation. Those thoughts made it really tough to finish my own letter.

After that macabre writing assignment was done, we loaded up the gear in my flat black PT Cruiser, Dean taking the front passenger seat. Fawn took JC and Sinera in her car, and we were off.

The trip was pretty silent, except for me trying to make some small talk to ease my nerves. No one bothered us as we drove to the dirt road intersection that would take us to the edge of the compound. We pulled into the trees and aimed our vehicles back down the road in case we needed a fast getaway. I was banking on that, actually. It'd mean we'd lived through the whole mess.

The night was cloudless. A waxing crescent moon hung in the sky. The temperature was cool enough to see our breath. The pine forest loomed above us, all-encompassing. Once under its needled branches, very little light reached the ground.

We went slowly and carefully, following Sinera's vague shape in front of us. The light grew brighter as we approached the edge of the cleared kill zone around the compound. It was easy to see — and intimidating. Searchlights from each tower swept the ground outside the fence. A visible glow came from behind the plastic covered hurricane fence, which meant a lot of lights were on. The towers made up part of the fence, so it would be easy to get up once we got to them. I asked myself for about the zillionth time: Why the hell did I agree to do this kind of job?

The searchlight swept regularly back and forth. Sinera scratched out a quick circle in the rocky soil. We stood close as she called power and chanted its shape. I felt a soft weight on my shoulders as Sinera finished the spell.

"Now move slowly, no faster than an easy walk. Any more with this many people, I will lose the spell, and we'll be seen."

Sinera then began a slow walk towards the tower. We followed in a tight cluster across the uneven ground between the trees and the fence. The twenty meters to the fence looked a mile away. The searchlight swept our way and Sinera slowed to a halt. We remained as close to her as possible.

The light tracked right across us as we stood unmoving. I thought it slowed as it played across us. Despite the suit, cold sweat prickled my skin, and my knees trembled. I was all ready to bolt when the bullets started flying, then the light passed over us and away across the ground. My stomach sank back out of my throat as we resumed the slow walk towards the tower. The light passed our way again, but searched behind us along the edge of the woods.

When we reached the tower, Fawn and Sinera started up the barbed wire-covered leg. Fawn grabbed the leg and slowly moved up, using the wire as a purchase for her shoes and gloves. Sinera began another soft chant, and the air sounds around us became fuzzy, like listening through a thick blanket.

Fawn reached the lip of the canvas cover. She gathered her legs under her, using the barbed wire as an anchor. How she got up all that loose wire was a feat in itself. I could see her lips move, but wasn't able to hear what she might have said.

Sinera was halfway up when Fawn launched herself under the canvas. The searchlight suddenly jerked back and forth wildly. Sinera scrambled up the leg, losing a piece of her clothing on the way up. She disappeared under the canvas. The searchlight began moving smoothly once again.

Fawn leaned out from under the canvas and dropped a knotted rope. JC grabbed it, and I heard the wood groan slightly as the Orc slowly pulled his bulk up to the canvas tower. Dean followed, agile as a squirrel leaping from tree to tree. I was last, and the rope was pulled up as I carefully used my feet to avoid the barbed wire on the tower leg.

I was helped by JC as I was pulled under the tarp. The searchlight poked through a cut slot in the canvas wall, and Sinera swung it back and forth, keeping in time with the other lights. The floor of the tower was a three-meter by three-meter square about five meters off the ground. The two cult members, wearing brown and green hunting camouflage, carried semi-automatic hunting rifles. Hopefully not too many of them had assault rifles like ours.

Personally, I didn't appreciate the distinction. Getting shot would be bad no matter what kind of rifle you were shot with. I looked over at Fawn, and those nagging fears came back. Before, it was all abstract fear of what might happen. Now, we were in it. We were looking Death very squarely in the face, and he was smiling. All those fears came back like a runaway freight train. I wanted to hide, but I couldn't. Fawn was here. I had to swallow my fear, and keep moving.

By the time I got my imagination under control, both men had been gagged with their ski masks, and bound with zip ties at the wrists and ankles. They weren't going anywhere. Fawn anchored the rope to an eyelet used to hold the searchlight on the platform. We went down in reverse order: Fawn going first, followed by me, Dean, JC, then finally Sinera. Sinera tied the rope to the barbed wire so it was partly camouflaged against the leg.

Fawn gathered us around in a quick huddle. "No going off on your own. Stay with your partner. I'll be hopping between you four as we go a little at a time through here. The building's we're going to look at first are the dark ones. Those are the most likely to hold Ginny. Last thing: no killing. You kill someone here and it doesn't matter what happens, you'll be going up on murder charges. I'm sorry, but that is what the law will say."

She looked at each of us in turn, then continued. "Okay JC, Dean, you're first. To the edge of that building, hold there. We'll move past you when you indicate the alley between the buildings is clear. Sinera, Fern, you stop at the edge of the next building and watch for those foot patrols Sinera saw. JC, Dean, ready …"

She paused a moment, then whispered.

"Go!"

# 20

DEAN AND JC MOVED SWIFTLY AND SILENTLY to the edge of the building. JC stayed flattened against the wall as Dean lay down and looked around the corner. He held a hand back towards us, two fingers raised. JC set his guitar case down next to Dean, then quietly leaned the FN-FAL against the wall of the building. He flexed his hands and crouched slightly. Dean kept watch for another minute, then waved us forward.

Sinera moved past them in a burst of motion easily twice what I could achieve. She lay on the ground by the next building, looking down the open ground between the buildings we were next to, at the row of plywood cabins three meters away.

I had the Howdah out, and in my hands.

Sinera whispered, "Please do not use that. Silence is our best ally."

I reluctantly slid it into my rear holster, and got one of the Sykes-Fairburns out. I really hoped it wouldn't be needed. I've been in exactly one knife fight, and it was only because Zhirk was there that I didn't get carved up like a Christmas pie. So, not a fun memory.

I heard footfalls on soft earth. They weren't worrying about being quiet. The irregular sounds said there were two.

Sinera glided to her feet, hands on her throwing knife bandoleer. I felt her relax as the sounds receded. The next building over was the first of two dark and locked buildings, if I remembered the layout JC had drawn. Then we could find out what was so important to lock up.

Sinera waved the others ahead. JC and Dean flashed by and stopped, pressing themselves against the wall. Fawn ran forward with them and then stopped with me and Sinera.

"Oh crap!" she hissed quietly, "Go prone."

We all dropped, and rolled tight against the base of the barracks. The sound of heavy footfalls approached us. The silence made them sound all the more ominous as they got louder. A human and a Hamref stepped around the corner of the building. They both had dark hunter's camouflage clothing. The human carried a lever-action rifle; the Hamref held a forearm long stick with a thumb-like cutout at the end. Six two-foot long barbed darts were held by clips on each of the Hamref's thighs. The stick was an *atlatl*, used to give leverage to spears so they could be thrown harder and farther. The darts would fit the *atlatl*, and the Hamref's long arms were an ideal lever for the thing. The barbs meant that the weapon was supposed to stick in the target. I wondered if the darts were poisoned.

They walked towards us, scanning the ground, the edges of the roofs, and out towards the woods. How they managed to miss us I didn't understand until I heard Sinera whispering. She chanted as quietly as she could while the two were near us. I'd remembered that now I didn't need a circle or a chant. I could have done something with my (relatively) new abilities. To back up Sinera, I built the idea of being unnoticed, of being just rock and leaves on the ground.

To say the power came to me was an understatement. Fawn was right next to me, and a flood of power erupted from her as I started the spell. The sensation was dizzying. I could taste, smell, and hear … everything around the spell's intent. It was ridiculously easy to control and tune the spell so completely that no one would look at us, even if we were naked, carrying pizza and beer.

Sinera choked off her chant. Her head whipped towards me in alarm as my spell settled over us like a shroud.

"Jeebus, Fern. What the hell?!" came Dean's sharp whisper.

He stopped and swung his weapon up with an *"Oh shit!"* and froze as the two guards chatted about the cold air, and how it would be nice to get off shift.

Dean's reaction should have alerted the guards, but they never looked our direction. Instead, they gazed at the open ground towards the fence, then shrugged and went down the path just in front of us.

"Damn, Ferny, what did you do to me? I feel weird."

Fawn stood up, and brushed herself off. The two guards turned the corner and disappeared from sight as JC and Dean started checking the few open windows. I was nearly drunk on the magick I'd pulled from Fawn. I knew I could keep this spell going indefinitely.

In the back of my mind, I knew how much power it took. It should have been way beyond me to keep up, but now I had so much power, it was a trivial task to maintain the spell. It was so natural, I didn't even wonder at this change.

Bolstered by the amazing success of the "Don't notice us" spell, we walked to the door. Light snow started falling as Dean beat me to the lock with his pick set.

"You just keep that spell up," Fawn said with a tinge of awe in her voice. "What have you been studying and who with? I could use some lessons like yours."

The lock clicked. Dean put his tools away and set up behind JC, who was busy slinging the FN-FAL back over his shoulder. He picked up his guitar case as Sinera set up on the opposite side of the steps.

Fawn pushed herself in front of the Elf. "I go in after JC opens the door, then JC. We alternate on down. No running. Go slow and quiet. We don't know how much noise Fern's spell can handle, so there's no reason to take chances right now."

The rest of us nodded silently. The magick rolled across my skin. It was, to put it mildly, distracting. The closest I can come to describing it is like being existentially caressed.

I squirmed in exquisite discomfort as JC turned the handle and Fawn stepped forward to push the door open and lean on it, holding it open. JC padded in to the left, the Orc scanning the room, looking for potential enemies. Sinera slipped past Fawn to the right, her hand up by her head with two blades in her delicate fingers. Dean followed JC and swept left, moving past the Orc deeper into the room. I walked to the right, past Fawn, then Sinera, until I was two-thirds of the way to the north wall. Sinera said something in Elvish. I recognized a curse when I heard it.

The room was filled with crude, wooden beds: three rows of twenty across the dark floor. Each bed had two meters of space all around them. Roughly half of the beds held young women from all the races. Each wore a ragged sackcloth dress. They were all unconscious.

"Look closely at the beds."

Sinera's bowstring taut voice startled me. I glanced at her, then went over to the bed she was facing. My eyes took a moment to spot the iron collar around the girl's throat. A short length of chain anchored the collar to the end of the metal frame that the malodorous mattress rested on. Despite the cold, she was barefoot and bare-legged. None of the women had blankets. One small potbelly stove at the center of the room radiated too little heat to fight off the chill.

I heard JC over on the other side of the barracks speaking to someone. The darkness reluctantly revealed a vague blob where he was. While I could hear him, I couldn't hear who he was talking to. Then I noticed the faint taste of magick. I was right next to it — right next to them. The spell emanated from the bed I was standing next to, and from the one to my left.

Sinera moved back towards the center of the room, turning slowly once she reached the potbelly stove. "Many silence spells are in here. They must be on the beds."

I went to the empty bed to my left and quietly slid the mattress to the floor. A sheet of plywood had kept the threadbare mattress from falling through the frame. On that plywood, was a pair of dark circles: one inside the other, with what looked like Latin words sandwiched between. I couldn't read them, but I could sense their magick with my own, which was another little trick I hadn't realized I could do. The silence spell was geared to stop any noise that occurred on the bed.

I sensed Fawn's anger, and that of the others, through the magick. It damped their muttered curses. Their anger, and disgust at the conditions the women were kept in, raised goosebumps. I moved past the woman, walking over to Sinera. JC held a thrashing woman down on the bed, talking softly and quietly. It didn't appear to be doing any good.

This place was for the men to enjoy themselves by raping the women. I wanted to throw up, and managed, by only great good fortune, not to. The spell would cancel noise, but not smell, and vomiting tends to be a social reaction like yawning. In a crowded mall, it can get ugly. It was one of the tricks Fawn tried, when we were younger, after watching an old movie about kids looking for buried treasure. To say it worked was an understatement. The mall had to cordon off most of the main walkway to clean it up — which took a couple hours.

I checked each occupied bed, but none of the women in here were Ginny. As much as it pained me to leave them, that's what I was planning to do. With discovering these conditions, Fawn had more than enough evidence to bring the wrath of the RCMP down on this place, and I knew she would. She pulled out her camera and risked being seen with a pair of flash pictures. She *wanted* these people. Hell, I wanted to be there. I wanted to watch her turn this place upside down, and see all these sick cultists thrown in jail.

Wanting to see justice done wasn't going to find Ginny. It was time to check the other barracks. I padded over to Fawn.

"We need to find Ginny, and soon. She's the objective here, sis. Come back or call for backup when we get her out."

Fawn's cheeks throbbed with strain as she clenched her teeth and nodded curtly. She didn't like leaving the girls chained up, but she did it. Ginny first, and then these prisoners second. Trying to get them out now would just get us all caught — and likely killed or chained to a bed. We slowly left the prison barracks. I went through the door first in a reverse order of our entry. When we got outside, we walked slowly to the second large barracks. This was like the first: heavy dark curtains over the small windows, and a single door to the inside.

Dean whistled softly as he looked at the door. A deadbolt were placed at both the upper third and lower third of the door. A simple push plate was at the middle. The door pushed inward, like the other prison barrack. Deadbolts are notoriously hard to pick. This was going to take time.

It took Dean a long while to get both deadbolts unlocked. We were all dreading what we might see in here. After the first building, our imaginations were running overtime.

When the bottom lock clicked, Dean rotated it slowly, then cursed. "Door's warped, the lock won't turn."

"Well, friend, let me in there, I think I can get it." JC reached over to grasp Dean's key blank and twisted it just as Dean whispered, "No!"

The lock clunked and the door swung open a few inches with a silenced rusty creak.

"What the hell?" came from inside.

Feet shuffled towards the door. Fawn crouched, focusing herself. A surge of vertigo disoriented me, like something was being pulled out of me. The tugging sensation came from my sister. She took a step and raised a finger to tap the door, which swung open and slammed against the wall hard enough to crack the door frame. My spell nearly collapsed with the burst of noise. I pulled at the power and drew more to strengthen it, causing Fawn to gasp and stumble just as she reached the startled guards.

I put all of my concentration to reinforcing the "Don't notice us" spell as Fawn slapped a punch away, breaking the man's forearm where she'd touched it.

He screamed and the spell swallowed the noise and spit it into me. The agony in the scream burned in my stomach. Fawn's kick to the guard's shin snapped his leg. The second guard, another Hamref, was frantically trying to set a dart in his *atlatl*, then dropped it as JC closed on him. Dean charged with the Orc, tackling the Hamref to the floor. JC leaned over and gave the Hamref a punch, knocking it out cold.

Fawn noticed the damage she'd done and slapped the man open-handed across the face. Her blow lifted him off his feet. He spun twice before he landed on the wooden floor, unconscious. Fawn grabbed the man's sawed-off shotgun, emptied it, then cut strips of cloth from his pants leg to improvise a splint for his shin. She zip-tied the other guard at the ankles and wrists. Once they were secured, we took the time to look at the interior.

# 21

THE ROOM WAS DIMLY LIT WITH PINK BULBS. Fifteen cribs were spaced much like the beds had been in the first room, with two meters separating each crib. In the center of the room, there was a table and three chairs. On the table lay a cribbage game, money, and cards.

Fourteen cribs held babies ranging from a newborn to close to a year. It was hard to tell. The babies had runes painted on them that glistened like fresh blood. These runes shifted, crawling on their skin. All the children were gaunt with malnutrition.

Two women were chained to beds nearest the table, which had a small potbelly stove next to it like the first prison. Both women were hugely pregnant. That got me thinking about Fawn again, and the baby. What did our pulling magick from each other do to it? Fawn didn't seem in distress, so maybe nothing.

But, I was now a little more reluctant to call on magick close to Fawn.

"These children are going to be part of a sacrifice." Sinera sounded absolutely certain.

"What makes you say that?" I asked her.

I dropped the "Don't notice us" spell. Keeping it up began interfering with the spells on the building. They were tuned to sound, others tuned to the door, and yet others linked to the cribs.

This one had a number of interlocked wards that my magick had started to interact with. Dismissing the spell allowed the wards to settle back to quiescence. I wondered why magick interacted with some, and put it down to similarity. One was to detect sound; the other to make it unnoticed. It was possibly a clash of competing forms.

A quick glance around showed me Ginny wasn't here. That meant we had to keep looking. I knew Fawn would really rather call down the lightning on this place. Whatever was going on was nothing like anything I'd ever wanted to see.

Cults? Yeah, they're usually crazy, but religious crazy — like only believing in a few paragraphs or words in the Bible, the Koran, or whatever. These guys were so messed up this looked like a cheesy cliché on a satanic cult from a B-movie. It would be ridiculously overdone if we weren't here experiencing all the horror right in front of us.

Dean was pale as he walked next to Fawn and whispered, "Hey Fawn? How about a new plan? This is getting so deep I think we have to modify our goal."

Fawn looked at Dean, then to the rest of us, and then took a deep breath.

"Okay, new plan. Dean, you and I will exfil the camp and call for backup. JC, Sinera, and Fern will find Ginny and get her free. Once we get hold of the RCMP, we'll re-infil the camp and rendezvous at the women's barracks. From there we will move the children to the women's barracks, and guard them and Ginny until the RCMP storms the camp." She looked at me, then at JC and Sinera. "Anyone, anything?"

No one said a word.

Fawn walked to the door, and pulled it open. "Okay, let's go. Good hunting."

We all nodded as the Fawn and Dean slipped out the door into the night. It was going to be rough. The children's barracks looked more secure, but moving fifteen babies would be easier than twenty emaciated women. The snowfall had increased while we were inside. Now thick, fat flakes fell in abundance, hitting the ground and melting, but more were falling than melting, and already small mounds of snow were beginning to build up.

That was going to be a problem. Making *us* unnoticeable is easy. Making tracks not noticeable is darn near impossible without using an illusion. It would have to be big to cover the area we'd be walking around, but any wards keyed to magick would get set off. We'd been lucky so far. There were a lot of wards on the babies, fewer elsewhere.

Illusions, though — big ones like what I was thinking of casting — were fragile. Sinera came up with a different solution.

"Why not start capturing the roving guards now? I've not noticed any form of regular communication. They do have radios, but we've not encountered any who have checked back in with a central security station."

As I thought about it, JC spoke up. "I don't know about that. The tower is going to be a dead giveaway. The light's not moving. It's only been about ten minutes, but I get the feeling our window of being quiet is about to run out."

Sinera nodded. "I had not considered the light becoming a liability. Humans are usually so good at ignoring signs that it did not occur to me to animate the device."

That got me into a push-ahead-fast mode. We needed to find Ginny *now*.

I moved away from Fawn, and re-cast the "Don't notice me". The power came, but from a distance, like whatever I had linked into was partly blocked by something. I felt a slight bit of relief that the power I'd connected with wasn't Fawn. It still worked, but somehow was not as complete.

"Something's different," I told them. "We need to go slow and careful. The magick's being interfered with somehow."

JC nodded, a slouching grin on his face. "Good to know, Ms. Fatelli."

We stepped out into the thick snowfall. The snow would muffle sounds which helped us, so we walked to the south, and towards the open end of the compound. Sinera had drawn two boxes on the map, calling them cabins. They were isolated on the western end of the compound, which made them a likely place to hold important prisoners. The cabins were exposed on all sides to view from the guard towers. It took us a couple minutes to traverse the one hundred meters to them, moving at a slow walk to avoid losing the spell.

It took a while to see the cabins through the snow. Each cabin was twenty meters from the fence, in a direct line north to south of each other, with forty meters between them. Both were lit on the inside, but the curtains weren't completely blacking out the light, which was the biggest help in spotting them as we approached. Both had single guards posted by the doors.

JC motioned for us to gather close. "Ms. Fatelli, what say I go visit the one cabin to the north, and you and Sinera visit this one? I'll bring Ginny back to you if I find her. If it gets bad, I'll let Mack go."

I shivered. I hoped nothing in that place was that dangerous. JC gave us a lopsided grin, then lumbered quietly off into the snow. Sinera watched him disappear amid the swirling flakes, then turned as I motioned to her.

"Let's see about the guard here. I'll keep the spell going, you knock him out."

Sinera nodded. "I will do that."

We moved through the swirling flakes and right up to the one guard, who was shivering and stomping his feet to stay warm.

"Wish I hadda beer right now," he muttered to himself as Sinera snuck behind him.

She raised her hand, then struck with a closed fist, bashing him just behind the ear. He crumpled to the ground. Sinera and I propped him up against the cabin wall. I picked up his pump shotgun and emptied the shells out of it, then put it, barrel down, under one arm. Sinera studied the door as I finished fitting the shotgun under the guard's arms.

"This spell on the door is unfinished."

That was kind of unusual.

"Unfinished? What do you mean: 'unfinished'?"

Sinera grimaced sourly at the door as I stepped up beside her.

"Look for yourself. It would be easier than trying to explain it in this weather."

She had the right of it there, so I opened my Sight to view what she'd been describing. Lines of power like strands of blood-soaked thread ran through the door, looping out and back like loose stitching. Incomplete runes became visible on the door and the walls of the cabin. As I looked at them, a picture in my mind started coming together, like pieces of a jigsaw puzzle. This wasn't a protecting or a ward to warn anyone, this was to bind whatever was placed in this cabin to here until the runes and the spell was completed.

The magick was all linked to blood, and that gave the spell its look, and told me of its purpose: to hold energy from beings from dissipating. It was a place set for some kind of ritual sacrifice. I closed the other Sight, letting a slight dizziness pass before I knelt at the door. Sinera kept watch while I pulled out my lockpick set and began to work the lock.

On a whim, I turned the doorknob first, and the door opened. It hadn't been locked. Inside were five bodies. They lay haphazardly on the floor, all of them inside a meticulously-drawn triangle inside a circle. Along each long side of the triangle were more Latin inscriptions. All the young-looking women had swirling runes painted on them, just like the babies. The chests of their bodies expanded and sank slowly. They were still alive, but sleeping or held unconscious.

With the circle, I thought the latter, though why put them here? Hold them until whatever spell was going to be cast was ready? No, it was preparation. The spell was going to be cast soon and this was the way of arranging everything so it went off without delay or interruption. That insight scared me. I counted the bodies. Five. All female. All under twenty, if I was guessing correctly.

None of this was in any way comforting. Sinera turned abruptly, bringing up a pair of knives. I started to reach for the Howdah inside the coat, then stopped and crouched. I would tackle him and let Sinera thump him quiet. At least that was the plan, until JC materialized out of the snowfall.

"Ginny's not there, but there are five nude young women over there in an odd-looking circle."

I gestured to the inside of the still open door. "Like that one?"

JC peered at the open doorway, then nodded. "Yeah, just like that one."

My stomach started rumbling. It didn't like the idea of ten people being sacrificed. Add that thought to the troubling one of the runes looking the same. Did that mean the babies were to be sacrificed the same way? I hoped not, but the evidence here was pointing in that direction pretty dramatically. The big question was: why were these out here, and the babies back in that large room? If the ritual was supposed to be in these cabins, why have them away from the site if you're readying it?

*That's because they're already in place, just like the ones here,* my paranoiac self replied.

"Ms. Fatelli, why are you scowling like that?"

JC's voice cut through the growing outrage in my mind and brought me back to the present.

The snow was half a shoe deep by now, and promising to get a lot deeper. I wished we'd have taken a look at the weather forecast before coming. The all-black ensemble was going to be very distinct against a white background. I poured more power into the "Don't notice me", and started towards the collection of cabins and barracks back to the north. If Ginny was going to be anywhere, she would be in those. I'd find her if I had to take each one apart.

We moved slowly forwards, keeping in what tracks we could find so our passing wouldn't look out of place. We got back to the baby prison, which is the only way I could think of it. It really was a sacrificial altar, but I didn't want that image in my mind. The cabins here were small, maybe five to six meters to a side. Most of them were lit. JC, being the tallest of the three of us, peered inside a window that had the shade only partly drawn down.

"Huh, just like the ones we just left. Only two in here though, both male. Young, I think. They've got tattoos also."

This was getting seriously creepy weird. Where were all the others? This place should have been filled with sleeping guards and workers. There should have been a main building of some kind, but the only two were a rape shed and a baby prison. It was baffling and sickening.

Sinera gasped as Fawn set her hand on my shoulder. I about jumped out of my skin, and JC spun with his guitar case raised to bash the intruder.

"Nice welcome," Fawn murmured quietly as we settled down.

Dean strode up through the swirling snow as JC lowered his guitar case.

"We got through, but it's going to take them time to get here. Lake Echo wouldn't do anything. Halifax is rolling now. They should be here in an hour, given the crappy weather and distance."

Fawn looked at the four of us. An hour would be too long if we were discovered. Based on Sinera's estimates, there were around forty armed men in this place. We'd knocked out two in the tower, two in the baby prison, and two more at the east end of the encampment. Six out of fifty. Not good odds, and we'd been lucky, even with the "Don't look at me" going. There were too many things that could go wrong, and Murphy's Law hadn't made an appearance yet.

Which meant it was only time before it did.

# 22

I LAID OUT WHAT WE'D FOUND SO FAR for Fawn and Dean. Dean got very quiet and stone-faced. Fawn's jaw muscles clenched and her eyes blazed. She was one step from losing it. Her cooler side prevailed after a moment, and she spit something dark like blood onto the snow.

"New plan. Check every cabin here. If you run into anyone walking around, knock them out. We'll talk to them after we finish checking the camp. This doesn't sound like what we expected here, and I want to know what is really going on. Spread out and check things." She looked over to me as I fidgeted. "Something to say, Fern?"

"If you find a girl with blonde hair and a French braid, call me or JC. We can tell you if it's Ginny or not." I finished with a description of Ginny's height and weight.

"All right, anything else?"

None of us answered, which was answer enough. The snow had slowed down some. We could see further, but so could the guards. Fawn nodded, then waved us out. We scattered slowly.

I cast the "Don't notice me" again and walked slowly through the accumulating snow towards the first cabin that no one had targeted. The cabin itself was about five meters by seven. The blackout shades were drawn, and the door was locked. I knelt at the door and unzipped my lockpicks. A few moments later, I had the lock turning.

I pushed the door slowly open, gritting my teeth, and hoping against a squeak. The door opened noiselessly. Inside was a bed on the left, a small refrigerator to the right, a stove next to the refrigerator, a few cabinets along the far wall, and a set of bunk beds further down the right side. This room had no circles or magick wards. I pulled the door closed, moved to the next closest cabin, and repeated the process.

The next cabin, which was smaller, more like three by three meters square, held three bodies of young men. Each had those greasy-looking, slowly shifting runes painted on them. The bodies were piled haphazardly in another circle with a triangle and Latin, just like the ones we'd seen before at the two eastern cabins.

Whatever was going on looked random, which completely confused me. Why is this compound so long when it'd be easier to make it square or circular? Where were all the cult members? We should be neck-deep in them.

Another mystery was the choice of victims: all women in a cabin, or all men. I'd not found a mixed set of victims. What could that mean, if anything? That the people doing this were prudes? It couldn't be that trivial, could it? Yeah, and I had all my fingers. The nub of my finger ached in the cold. Phantom pain can be a bitch.

I moved slowly forwards as we checked the last houses. The snowfall had begun to thicken once more. If this kept up, we were in for a real heavy blanket of the stuff by morning. I thought it a minor miracle the guards in the stands hadn't tried to challenge us — black shapes on white snow and all that. We'd taken out six of them, which was about the number of guards patrolling the grounds that Sinera had mentioned. Had we taken them all out?

Dean was checking the last cabin, the westernmost one. He knelt and began picking the lock as I walked slowly up behind him.

"Anything yet, Dean?"

He didn't pay attention to me; his focus was completely on the lock, which clicked a moment later. He twisted the lock slowly, then pushed the door open. Dean peered in, then turned his head to look back at us, a sour smile on his face.

"And here she is. How crazy is it the last building on the site has her, and it's the one closest to the tower we used to sneak in. We should have checked this one first, and saved ourselves all that trouble"

He pushed the door fully open and stepped back. Ginny was in there alone, lying in a seven-pointed star surrounded by a circle with Latin scrawled out all around it. The room had another one of those pink lights. The walls had wards anchored by casting circles on each one and the ceiling. The little I did understand was that Ginny — her essence — was to be kept here by the wards.

Sinera touched my elbow as she moved up to observe the situation. Fawn and JC footfalls crunched lightly as they stepped on the light snowpack. We were all so noticeable, I was surprised that the other towers hadn't alerted to us and started shooting.

Ginny was like all the others: in a dirty sheet roughly cut to be a covering, slimy runes that moved all over her as we watched. The faint rise and fall of her ribs that meant she was alive. I was tempted to just run in and pick her up, but the oddness of the situation made me hesitate. Why all this preparation and no real trouble? The towers aimed out at the woods, but surely one or two would check the camp on occasion, if only to look at where they'd get hot drinks and a warm bed.

I rubbed the nub of my pinky finger as I thought about it. Maybe I was projecting myself too much into the guards, expecting them to do what I would, rather than what they would naturally do. Fanatics are people with an enthusiasm all out of proportion with reality. That's not bad: it can make you enjoy what you're doing, like watching Canadian Football and cheering your favorite team on.

Religious fanatics take it to a different level. Everything is built around their particular belief or leader. Rigid adherence to rules makes them incapable of seeing beyond the limits of their own beliefs. So maybe they were just as fanatical about spotting enemies and, since they're in the towers, their job or mission was to detect anyone coming out of the trees. I shook my head. If it was that simple, then these men were stupidly rigid.

It didn't matter in the end. Our job was done. Now we had to get Ginny out. I started up into the room, then the next thing I remember is waking up on my back outside the cabin and Fawn slapping my cheek.

"Shorty, you really have to quit being so impulsive," Fawn growled at me, then hugged me tight. "You took one step past the door and dropped like a puppet with its strings cut. Thank gods that your legs were close enough to the door to grab without going inside to get you."

Sinera spoke up after Fawn finished the hug. "There were alarms set with the wards. No one here has noticed, so wherever the alarm is, we can expect trouble very soon." Sinera checked her knife bandoleer again. "I do not believe we'll get out without combat."

Fawn clenched her jaw. "It'll be at least a half-hour before the MaRS team can get here. Let's stick to the plan, gather the babies up, move them to the women's barracks, lock the door, and hold out until then."

The nub of my finger ached, and so did the scars on my ribs. The cold air made them feel like they were being dipped in molten glass. I bit my lip to keep from screaming. Sinera made a quick circle in the snow as Fawn helped me up. I watched the Elf scratch a series of runes inside the circle with one of her knives. She then drew a smaller circle inside the runes. Sinera chanted softly then leaned forward in her circle and made a pushing motion at the cabin.

There was a shuddering sensation that made the cabin rock slightly, and my skin goose-bumped at the release of the magick wards. Something two cabins to the right of us flashed brightly, and a wolf's howl lifted in the air. Shouting started up in the towers.

Sinera didn't hesitate. She leapt into the room, gathered Ginny in her arms, and staggered out. She stumbled over to JC. "You carry her," she grunted, then dropped Ginny in JC's surprised arms.

Not bothering to check if JC actually caught Ginny, Sinera streaked off over the snow at a speed I could only imagine. She sidestepped as a bullet hit the snow to her right, and let fly a pair of knives she had in her fingers.

The knives must have hit their target; a scream came from the tower. JC cradled Ginny and his guitar case in the same arm, and did a fast trot towards the two large barracks. Other shouts and gunfire started up. The big Orc hunched over and did his best to shield the unconscious Ginny with his own body from any incoming bullets. It brought a lump to my throat how much he looked like Zhirk at that moment.

Sinera threw again, and a second scream of pain came from the tower. She sprinted towards the one tower in the center of the north wall, grabbing at her bandoleer, then holding her arm low and away as she started dodging back and forth. That's when the snow really started to fall.

The heavy flakes cut down all vision to about four meters. I knew I was heading in the right direction, but the wall suddenly looming out surprised me and I skidded to a stop, struggling to reorient myself.

Dean staggered by, a bullet striking the wall near him. How could those guys see him? I couldn't see the towers through the snow.

I ducked and moved with Dean, sliding between some of the cabins and working through the jumble towards the two barracks. I heard faint screams between the sharp reports of rifle fire and throatier shotgun blasts. Fawn mumbled to herself and threw a hard kick at the baby door. The door, unlocked from the last time we visited, swung open so hard the upper hinge tore loose from the frame and slammed heavily into the wall, the doorknob bulging wood outwards from the impact.

A heavy pull tugged at something in me as Fawn kicked. The sensation felt like a slight release of pressure of an opening sinus after a head cold. I shook the feeling off as Fawn came back out, cradling two babies, who suddenly began to writhe and squall when they felt the cold began to nip at them.

JC, still cradling Ginny and his guitar, followed Fawn while Dean and I went into the cabin and each scooped up two more babies. The sensation of the runes slithering along my skin creeped me out, but I wasn't thinking of much at the moment beyond moving the babies to the other barracks where we'd all be safer. Another pair of screams, more gunshots a distance away from us, and Sinera came staggering back holding her leg.

She had a number of small holes in it, and both forearms, with blood leaking from all of them.

"Shot is difficult to dodge," she said matter-of-factly. Her calm voice was at odds with her pale skin and pain-filled eyes.

I wanted to take the time to perform a healing. Having Sinera healthy for what was going to come — whatever it was — could make the difference between succeeding or dying. The flip side was I didn't have any confidence that healing could be done that fast or completely.

Fawn took one look at Sinera and pointed at the women's prison barracks. "You're in there. Bandage that up, rest, and be ready if things change. We'll be with you shortly."

Sinera nodded, then hobbled to the barracks without a word.

# 23

As Sinera moved away, JC sidled up next to me. "You keep your head down, boss. We're getting bad company soon. I heard a car a little bit ago and, according to your sister, it's way too soon for MaRS to get here. You'd think they'd send MaRS teams via portal."

I agreed with JC, but Fawn had said that portal work is exhausting to all involved. Unlike the military, that has a whole section dedicated to magick combat and use, the RCMP is more about reaction to a crime, which generally has almost no time to prepare a minimum of eighteen mages, identify the location, and send up to nine people through. It's great for short-notice things, if you're prepared ahead of time, but that kind of coordinated magick is limited pretty severely when all you have is a minute, or less, to respond.

A typical limit that the RCMP has, when they have the resources, is about fifty kilograms per wizard. So a group of ten prepped wizards could send a squad of five people of around one hundred twenty kilograms a piece, including equipment, through a portal.

There's a lot more to it, but that's the general idea: it's delicate, needs preparation time, a known location, and enough wizards to transport the total amount of mass. It's not easy to set up outside of military ops. That being said, it still would been nice if the RCMP could send the whole MaRS team here. I'd like our chances a lot more with them around. Be that as it is, they were going to be a while, and we had to find a way to hold out long enough.

All the thoughts about holding out vanished with the roar of an angry Troll. My courage sank into my shoes and whimpered, trying to hide. Fawn kicked it into high gear.

"Grab the babies now! JC, you're the toughest nut we have. If that Troll shows his head here, do your best to take it off. The rest of you, get those kids moved!"

JC didn't look at all the easy-going Orc he'd been most of the time. Now a scowl sat on his features. His broad mouth curled like a dog's snarl, revealing his large, spiky teeth. He loped in the direction of the roar. I guess it was to scout out what was coming in addition to the Troll.

Fawn smacked me on the back of my head, knocking my thoughts away from watching JC run towards trouble. We began shuttling back and forth between the two barracks as fast as we could. By a small miracle we got all the babies transferred before the first shots rang out.

The *crack!* of the hunting rifle was followed by a shout, then another angry roar from the Troll. I couldn't see what was happening; the snow was still coming down thick and fast. Fawn herded us into the women's barracks. Each child had been placed with one of the chained women. Sinera had been moving to each bed, destroying the circles under the mattresses and the ones under the beds. The place reeked of raw magick as the circles emptied themselves. The magick was not dissipating like expected. Rather, it was being held and concentrated. Sinera continued to break the circles by cutting through them with her silvery-looking throwing blades. She finished up and sneezed, then clutched her still-oozing leg. I stepped over to her, and placed a hand on her shoulder, turning her towards a chair.

"Sit down and let me look at your leg again. I've got a small first aid kit. Let's get the wound properly wrapped."

Sinera looked at me like she wanted to argue, then a baby's wail sounded, startling the both of us. One baby started another, who began to cry as well ... which started another, and another, until they all were wailing at the top of their lungs.

Sinera limped over to the chair, sinking heavily onto it. She looked back at me, then said, "I believe there was milk substitute in the other building."

A couple more shots rang out, followed by staccato bursts from an assault rifle. Rifles and shotguns answered, making the area sound like a war zone. It likely was. Then I heard what I never wanted to again: the high-pitched giggle of JC's "Shambler", Mack. The eerie wail from the creature threatened to freeze the blood in my veins.

There came a scream, and its giggling ratcheted up into a full maniacal wail. I heard the Troll bellow and the creature giggle madly. JC returned at a full run, literally leaping through the door. He dashed around the room, pulling the blackout curtains across the windows.

"Kill those lights; they're coming. I counted fourteen, including the Troll and a pair of Troykin. Mack won't be able to stop them," he said rapidly, as he continued pulling down the shades.

Fawn didn't bother looking for a light switch. She swung the butt of her assault rifle and smashed each light. The magick started to slowly dissipate once the lights were destroyed.

"The circle was painted on the light, then the spell linked to activate when the light did. The color was used to trap the magick in a projected circle. It is my belief that now the magick is diminishing in here," Sinera explained like a college professor.

For some crazy reason, her speech made me wonder why, in all the places, she decided on being a secretary. A question for later, to be certain, but it really rankled me that I didn't realize that she was hiding her skills and abilities so well. I suppose I should have looked at her with the mage Sight, but I'm not one that really relies on magick all that much. It had just never occurred to me.

The blood-curdling tittering from the Shambler rose in volume. I heard a faint, choked scream, and the Troykins started making a noise like a coyote trying to cough and howl at the same time. The tittering reached a pitch so high that I couldn't hear it, but I felt my spinal cord resonate with it. The sense of dread and fear was overwhelming.

Dean dropped to his knees, hugging himself in terror. Fawn stood, locked rigid by the barely registering sound. The tittering became a shriek, like glass shattering. Then the roar of the angry Troll started echoing once more.

JC pulled the guitar out and left the case open. He set the guitar aside, checked his assault rifle, then thrust a hand into his pocket, pulling out cartridges, and started refilling the clip while he looked through the small window.

I tried to throw up after that hideous wail stopped, but my stomach settled for dry heaves. It was in our favor that they didn't quite know where we'd gone. The thick snowfall kept visibility short, and that helped us. What didn't was the wailing of the babies. There was no way we could get back over to the other barracks and bring back enough bottles and formula for the babies with the cult members out there looking for us in this jumbled bunch of cabins.

I sat down and started working on a big "Don't notice anything here" casting. I wanted a circle for this, so I opened the pouch with the chalk, pulled the piece out, and began quickly sketching a crude circle on the floor.

The circles don't have to be perfectly round to work. They can be almost any shape, provided there's no break in the line. A circle is what most people use because it doesn't have a weak spot like the corners of a triangle does. Magick energy would gather at the weak spots and eventually leak out. Circles, without corners, distribute the pressure of the magick equally, along the line. That's why they're preferred over designs with corners.

I finished the circle, dashed in a few symbols for focus and control, then sat and tried to pull power as fast as I could. Fortunately for me, a lot of unfocused power was available due to the former circles holding power. I got some from the room, but there was that odd link through which a dizzying amount of power flowed. Fawn gasped, and I reveled in the sheer volume I had to use. It was the simplest thing to brute force a "Don't notice this" ward around the entire building.

Before all the weirdness in PEI, I would have been at that circle for hours to get the same result, and here I was simply willing it into being. I had no idea why and, truthfully, I didn't care one bit. Knowledge is power, but magick is power too. And I had magick now. Big-time magick. Magick ability enough to pull power and shape it without needing a circle. Larry didn't need one, but he used it often, as he liked the greater focus and control.

I held the spell in place and anchored it to the crude circle. It wouldn't last but a day or two at the most, then the magick would be leaking out of the circle and the spell would dissipate.

It would be long enough if nothing attacked the spell directly. And yeah, I mentioned that because, ten minutes later, that's what happened.

A Troykin stumbled into the spell by accident. His natural magick null brought the casting down when he ran into it. There were shouts of surprise as the wailing babies weren't hidden by the "Don't notice this" spell. Just as I'd gotten it up, the spell collapsed on me. A lone figure heaved into view.

JC didn't wait, and shot the Troykin. The three-round burst was loud in the open room. I heard the Troykin howl with pain. I don't know if that meant he was dead; I rather hoped he was still alive. We didn't want a murder accusation directed at us.

Another human ran towards the building, then tried to turn and duck low to avoid being shot. JC shot at him anyway. There weren't any howls of pain, so he probably missed. The door shuddered with a loud thump. One of the cultists was trying to force his way inside. JC started for the door, but Fawn beat him to it.

She waited for the next crash against the door, then yanked it open. The startled cultists fell forward. Fawn slammed the door shut on two of the three, holding them jammed in place while she kicked their heads with her combat boot.

The third, a Hamref, hit the door, knocking Fawn backwards a step. She recovered her balance, then the magick was pulled from me. Fawn, for lack of a better way to describe what happened, powered up. She straightened, her eyes locking on the Hamref. A quick, skipping step brought her to the wide-open door. She pulled her leg up and threw a classic *tae kwan do* side kick.

The Hamref crossed his arms to block, which he did, but Fawn's power blew him out the doorway like a missile. He flew four meters in a straight line, and then crunched deafeningly through the walls of the other barracks. The other two men struggled to stand up. She flipped them both down the steps with a nudge of her foot and slammed the door closed.

JC was back at the window, giving Fawn a grim smile and a quick thumbs up. Dean was covering another window while I was laying out clips on a towel so whoever ran out of ammunition could reload easily. I pulled the Howdah out, then realized an important fact I hadn't thought of. Everyone in this group was right at or taller than one-point-eight meters, except yours truly.

The base of the windows was set at just under two meters off the floor to discourage escape attempts. I wasn't tall enough to see out. The barracks were made with raised floors, which meant there'd be room under the buildings for someone like me. That was the non-magick me thinking. The magick side knew that going outside was just a form of suicide cloaked in "being useful". I could be useful in here.

I got to work, sitting back down in the crude chalk circle by the fire. I focused, calming myself despite the shrieks of the frightened women and babies. I reached for power, and what flowed back was glorious! I got power from the room, pulling magick that smelled like my sister, and from something deep underneath the ground.

The last had such a dark power to it that I was giddy. You'd think I'd have been terrified, but it was like mixing coffee and alcohol: you get a wide-awake drunk. I was so besotted by the power I reeled. It was so simple to turn that power over: give it an emptiness on one side, and a physical hardness on the other. The barrier burst forth from me, covering each window and the one door in shimmering, pulsing color.

A bullet struck the door and stopped, sandwiched between shattered wood and the colorful ward. I could hold this for a while, but it needed constant power from me to keep its form. The minute I let the image go in my mind, it would drop.

The power was intoxicating. I laughed as bullets hit the spell, the impact tickling my skin. Once they hit the barrier, the bullets stuck against it, like metal flies on a shimmering flypaper. Dean crossed himself and looked over at me.

JC chuckled. "That is a pretty slick bit of work, boss. Keep it up and we'll be back home for a steak dinner."

Of course, no bit of optimism was going to go unpunished. It was at that time the cult's mages got into the act. The first magick bolt hammered me like a baseball bat upside my head; the second was a vicious repeat of the first. I kept the barrier up, but it was more through groggy instinct than me actually focusing. The third blow shattered it. I fell to my hands and knees, gasping in pain as the shock of the spell breaking lit up my nerves. My head ached, as did my body.

Ginny had awakened at some point. She huddled by the pot-belly stove, watching the proceedings with wide eyes. When I fell, she moved next to me and laid her hand on my head. She gasped as if burned, then suddenly my pain vanished.

I could feel her literally in my head. I could see her as she held her hand against my forehead. She glowed. I saw purity in her that went beyond words. I think "purity" might be the wrong word, but I can't think of any other word or description that fit my vision of her at that moment. She made things better.

It was a burst of cool, refreshing rain. My body threw off all the accumulated pain and cold and fear. I could do anything or, at least, I thought I could. I surged back to my feet as Ginny removed her hand.

The circle, by some small favor, had not gotten smudged through all the chaos. I sat down in it once more and focused on pulling power and feeding it into the barrier. The whirling colors sprang forth again just as the Troll launched himself at the door. He rebounded backwards. The surprised yelp was music to my ears. Then the casters got going again.

Their bolts hammered at me. Ginny saw what was happening, and put her hands on the back of my head. The pummeling pain flowed away, but I heard Ginny cry out as she absorbed the brunt of it. A second blow did the same, and this time Ginny didn't manage to stay in contact. She slumped to the ground, and landed on the circle.

The spell blew, forcing its way out the open windows and tearing through the rotted plywood at the window near Dean. Dean didn't wait for things to clear. He hosed the area in front of the open hole. Screams of rage answered the bullets that carried their lethal "To Whom It May Concern". The strikes and roars meant Dean had shot the Troll. I hoped he'd hit him hard, otherwise we were about to have a very short life.

Fawn dropped her rifle, and charged the door as the blood-mad Troll tore it off its hinges. The sudden pull at me was like a floodgate had been opened. It poured out of some place in me like a raging torrent and roared into Fawn. She actually braced the Troll, hand to hand, just like Amazons in the comics. I think everyone stopped and watched in awe as Fawn forced the Troll backwards, then kicked him out the huge opening where the door used to be.

She followed him outside. Two screams were followed by sounds like rotten wood snapping. Bullets tore through the long east wall, hitting one of the women. She grunted, then flailed, falling out of the bed. The baby she'd huddled around, trying to protect, lay still next to her, blood oozing from an eye socket. Another cultist tried to get inside the building. Fawn stepped over and grabbed his jacket from behind and pulled him out the door. He screamed for a second then hit the other barrack's wall with a splintering thud. Fawn stepped back through the door and slid to the scanty cover that the potbelly stove afforded her.

"IDIOTS! Don't shoot in there! They are necessary!"

Cameron's voice cut through the gunfire and the screaming babies.

The guns outside stopped. JC kept looking for targets as the cultists retreated into the thick falling snow.

"They are necessary. If there are any dead, you will need to draw straws to see who replaces them."

That made our choice of making a stand here a bit safer … relatively.

Fawn let the power drop. I felt a giddy backwash of released power. It was like we were linked. I stared wide-eyed at Fawn, who was looking at me in the same way. We'd never had anything like this happen between us before. It was like we knew everything the other was thinking, truly linked like twins. It bolstered us. We were ready to keep fighting.

But Cameron had different plans.

# 24

"HELLO THE CABIN! May I enter? I'm coming under a flag of truce."

JC stared out the small indow, then grunted, "Cocky bastard, just standing there."

He looked over at me and Fawn. This was Fawn's call. Sinera lay slumped, unconscious, next to the potbelly stove. Ginny looked groggy, but willing to fight. Tough girl that one.

I think both Fawn and I wanted to sleep until Spring, after all the magick we had thrown around, but that was more from the adrenalin drop than magick fatigue. Dean and JC were untouched, but we had three women with bullet wounds, and two dead— the woman and the baby I saw earlier.

"What do you think, Fawn? Should we even give him the time of day? I vote to let him freeze out there."

I was getting my second wind, and that brought clarity back to our predicament. I was frightened. We couldn't get this lucky twice. Cameron had some good mages out there — at least two, possibly more. If Sinera wasn't in such bad shape, we might have had an even shot at taking the casters out, but just Fawn and I … we didn't like our chances.

Oh sure, we had been supercharged, but with only two of us against three or four wizards, we'd likely lose. Add in the fact that neither of us had really studied magick, and the odds stacked worse. We were going by instinct, and it'd worked for us so far, but against mages who knew what they were doing was a totally different beast.

"I think, Shorty, that we invite him in and stall. The more time we waste talking, the closer MaRS gets to us." She shrugged and looked around the barracks at the huddled bodies, and the wailing babies. "He's got all the cards: we don't know where his mages are, or how many. We can break out of here, but the firepower out there could well get us killed trying to go for help."

It sounded like she was throwing in the towel without taking a shot first. I didn't like it. This was Fawn the Amazon, registered trademark pending. She'd just gone hand-to-hand with a freaking Troll and won! What is she doing, saying we're in the deep end?

Then I took a look around. Dean was on the floor. He was alert, but he had a sense of defeat to him. He acted as if this was the last stand. It took me a moment to put the two and two together. We couldn't save these people if we wanted to survive. Fawn was determined to protect them.

The women being chained to the beds offended her — and me — beyond words. Charging out to take the cultists on head-to-head on would get us killed, and them. Fawn couldn't do that. She couldn't leave them behind, and I couldn't leave Fawn behind. Sinera was still unconscious. We couldn't leave her either. The one person with the best chance was JC. But if he did take off,

Cameron and his cultists would shoot him down in a heartbeat. Even if he did manage to kill a few cultists, Cameron could always get more believers. Fawn was right: stalling was our only real option. The more we stalled, the closer MaRS got to us.

Another thought occurred: What if Cameron had a time limit too? If he was, that might be something we could exploit.

Apparently impatient with our lack of response, Cameron shouted, "I am still waiting, people. We can parley, or we can start shooting again. There's no way out of there, not without getting killed. You're completely surrounded. My mage 'friends' can do very unpleasant spells. It would be a shame to resort to that. I'm certain we can come to some agreeable terms without further bloodshed."

The creepy part was how he sounded so reasonable, so peaceful. A wave of disgust and anger rolled through me. How could he be so calm about this? How could he do this to other people? He needed to be taken out. My anger didn't hide the fear. What would he do to us if we did surrender? What if this was a trick?

I was still playing "what if?" in my head when a hard slap spun me halfway around. Fawn raised her hand to slap me again, then lowered it as I focused on her.

"Fern, he's been waiting a full minute. What do you say? Do we reject the talk? Or let him come talk with us?"

Fawn was ready to tell him to come in. I could see that in her eyes. Anything to buy time. Me, I was afraid there was a trick we missed. But there really was only one option: stall.

"Let him in. You handle the negotiations. This is more your expertise than mine."

Fawn nodded, and I could see JC and Dean relax. Ginny was over by Sinera, stroking her leg. Sinera's face was taut with pain as Ginny continued to run her hand up to Sinera's thigh, and back down to her ankle. The scene was disturbingly intimate to me, despite the desperate circumstances.

I was about to tell Ginny to quit, when I saw a few tiny black beads emerge from Sinera's wounds and then drop to the floor with a slight clatter. Then a few more. A moment later, it sounded like rain. Then, finally, one last light tap on the floor.

Ginny looked over at me. "It was steel shot. She was being poisoned by it. I got it out, but she's still sick."

"I'm still here and, if you don't answer, I will be forced to accept the answer for a peaceful negotiations is 'no'. So, if you are going to negotiate, please answer promptly." Cameron's voice carried easily through the falling snow.

I thought about what Fawn said.

"You're the one who knows about this. I'd rather not negotiate, but that's the selfish answer. I think you're right that we have to. It's the only way right now to have a chance."

Fawn nodded. "I'll do the best stall job I can and hope the cavalry gets here before things go bad."

JC smiled grimly and checked his pockets. He removed the clip from the rifle, then knelt, cradling the rifle as he fed cartridges into the thirty-round magazine. Dean kept a sharp eye out the window he was near, seeking movement in the snow. Fawn stepped to the wrecked doorway.

"All right, we'll negotiate. Come up here alone, and un-armed," Fawn shouted into the snowy darkness.

"I can do that," came Cameron's reply.

He gave in so easily that that there just had to be some kind of game being played. No one sounds so unconcerned without a reason. I immediately thought we were being conned.

Fawn thought the same way. "If anyone moves out there, or tries to get closer to the barracks, I'll shoot them."

"Understood," Cameron replied blithely. "We won't shoot, or try anything." He paused for a moment. "You know this situation doesn't have to be this hostile. We could sit down over some hot food and discuss our troubles, and see about finding a way around them … find a compromise."

He sounded like one of those television preachers.

Cameron approached, appearing out of the snow. His long, confident stride made him look all the more televangelical. The only thing he was missing was the bright, sequined suit and a Bible done up in glossy white that he could wave while misquoting it. He then walked between the two barracks to stand in front of the wood steps up to the wrecked wooden door and frame. He held out his arms and began a slow spin, showing that he had no weaponry.

"As you can see, I am unarmed, and alone."

I didn't believe "unarmed" for a second.

Fawn didn't either. She stared hard at the man, then said harshly, "Come up the steps to the top one and stop. You're not welcome inside."

Cameron's easy smile became brittle and fixed. He did as ordered, and climbed the steps to the top one in front of the gaping hole where the door used to be.

He looked at Fawn. I got the sense of two dogs sizing each other up. Cameron wore a thick olive drab parka. His hands were stuffed in its fleece-lined pockets. On his head was a heavy woolen black tuque — a wool cap with tassels. In spite of the heavy garments, the cold and snow discomfited him.

Fawn stared grimly at Cameron. She was in full cop mode, and he was the perp. It didn't matter that we were surrounded, and outgunned. There were people here — women and babies — that needed protecting, and, by all the powers that be, Fawn would protect them.

Cameron frowned. I don't think he expected someone as focused as Fawn.

"Hold out your arms." She wasn't going to give him time to think.

Cameron did so and Fawn stayed inside the doorway and methodically patted him down for hidden weapons: squeezing his forearms and biceps, patting along his ribs and stomach, down each leg to the ankle, then reaching up between his legs to check his groin.

Cameron had lost all sense of humor. His features had grown tense with held-back anger at being treated like a criminal.

I think both Dean and JC got a kick out of it. They were both smiling as Fawn finished her check, obviously enjoying Cameron's discomfort. Cameron stood there, his frown growing deeper with each passing moment. The fat flakes blew in front of his face, some fluttering along the skin before sticking and melting, some impacting his wool cap, freezing in its black tufts.

"Is this for your amusement? Should I turn and leave? Or just tell my men to start shooting?" He looked like he was very willing to go down in a blaze of friendly fire if we went with him.

Fawn caught on that she'd pushed it far enough, and yanked him into the room. I saw Cameron's eyes widen as Fawn lifted him off the ground with one hand. She turned, and dropped him on the floor close to the potbelly stove.

"Now that you're here, sit down and let's talk."

Fawn escorted him over to the rickety card table and slid a folding chair over for him to sit in. Cameron sat down, still angry. Fawn remained standing. Her hands hung loosely at her sides, ready for use. Cameron crossed his own arms as he sat upright in the chair. He coughed, bringing a hand up to his mouth, then put his hands in his lap and returned Fawn's gaze with a smile that didn't reach his eyes.

"Yes, let's talk. I'm all for peaceful negotiation if it will save lives. We're not enemies. If you surrender, you'll be treated fairly and released in a few days."

His demeanor changed as he talked, becoming more open and personable. Everything sounded so reasonable that I had a flash of doubt that he knew anything about what was happening here.

One of the women sat up from the bed nearest the stove, and stared at Cameron's back. Her eyes went wide with hate as she crept off the bed. She stopped and spun when Ginny grabbed her shoulder, her fist raised to strike. Ginny and the women stared at each other, then she quietly returned to her bed, her eyes on Cameron like he was a snake coiling on the floor.

"No, I don't think that's going to work. That doesn't do anything for all of us here. You didn't guarantee their release, nor the children's. They go free, with no interference; the children go with them. You have your men lay down their arms, surrender, and then you'll get a fair trial and fair treatment."

Cameron smiled. I brought up my Sight. His hand glowed a dull brown as my eyes focused. He saw my eyes widen. Fawn saw both our reactions and moved. Power suddenly flowed from me, and elsewhere. It went to Fawn, who moved so quickly she just flickered like an afterimage.

One moment she was standing, the next she had Cameron's hand clenched closed with her own, his arm at full extension. He gasped in pain as she twisted the hand back to weaken the grip, then somehow slid her fingers inside his closed fist. She pulled the item loose, holding it in her own hand as she swept his right foot off the ground. Rotating his arm, she forced him into a kneeling position, his arm twisted and bent behind him.

"JC, could you take over on his arm? Dean, move the chair over to JC's window for Fern, she can keep watch while we talk with our prisoner."

JC cracked his knuckles and strode over to Cameron, who got wide-eyed as the Orc's large hands settled on his twisted arm and gave it a small tug. Fawn kept her one hand clenched around whatever she'd gotten away from Cameron. She held her closed hand in front of his face.

"What is this thing?" Fawn demanded.

When Cameron didn't answer immediately, she looked up at JC, then back to Cameron.

"You can talk or, I swear to God, I'll tell JC to rip your arm from the socket, and I'll ask the question again."

Cameron grew wild-eyed as JC increased the tension on the arm. The Orc was easily strong enough to do just what Fawn had suggested.

As a cop, that had to go against what she believed in. At the same time, there wasn't anything about situations like this, and Fawn wasn't here as an officer.

"RELEASE! me and I'll tell you."

# 25

J C RELEASED CAMERON and let him stand up. Cameron looked around, then straightened his coat. It bothered me a little, but I didn't think much of him being uncontrolled. Cameron looked around, then straightened his coat.

"Hand the charm back to me."

Fawn gave him the charm. I continued to look out the window. He'd not talked to me directly, so it was all good as far as I was concerned.

"Put your weapons down."

We all did it in unison. There wasn't any reason not to. He wasn't the enemy. Ginny was wide-eyed at the sudden change, but remained frozen on her knees next to Serina. He looked around at the women.

"Take the children back to their cribs, then lock yourselves back to your beds." He thought for a moment. "The ones furthest from the stove."

The women staggered upright, moving their malnourished bodies, carrying the quiet babies back to the other barracks. We waited until they returned a few minutes later, pale and shivering, then moved to the beds against the walls of the barracks, and voluntarily clamped the silver and iron collars around their throats.

Cameron smiled. "Now lie down and wait."

Everyone lay down. We were still waiting to see what he needed from us. Since we hadn't been addressed, we hadn't moved. I still stood on the chair, looking out the window on tip-toes, waiting for my next action. Cameron shrugged deeper into his thick parka.

"Ginny, come here."

The girl shifted a moment, then stood up. She walked over to Cameron and faced him. Her features appeared completely serene, like we all were. He swept his gaze over all of us, then settled on Fawn.

"Strip naked, and chain yourself to a bed."

Fawn shrugged out of her insulated suit and complied, locking the metal collar around her neck like the others. He motioned at Dean and JC.

"You two, strip naked and go out to the others. Bring them here."

JC took off his black ensemble, his green-gold skin glowing in the few remaining lights. Dean finished stripping and the two wandered out into the snowstorm. That left me, Ginny, and Serina alone with Cameron. He smiled, then laughed out loud.

A moment later, JC and Dean reappeared, leading eleven others armed with rifles and shotguns. I hadn't dropped my

Sight yet. The last four in the group had a stronger glow about them. Mages. They weren't powerful, but there were four.

Mages like myself, Fawn, and the like can cast a large number of small spells, but practiced casters, like our parents, could — and did — conjure major workings. A team of casters multiplies their power, rather than simply adding it together. A good coven of witches or casters can do serious damage, as the world found out when The Change happened. Most of Canada is now dangerous to travel through, and the U.S. west of the Ohio River is that way too. The world here is way different than it was, take it from me.

Once all the men were gathered together, Cameron looked at the others. "You go check the other cabins. Make sure they're all undisturbed. Tonight is auspicious. We've got everything we need."

He looked at us. JC and Dean shivered, still naked, waiting for their next orders. Fawn lay on the bed near the stove; Cameron hadn't specified where. I still stood on the chair, and still on my tip-toes looking outside. I'd seen movement, but no one asked me to report it. My calves burned from being on my toes for so long, but it wasn't important. I just continued to do what I'd been tasked with last.

Then came my first order. "Ms. Fatelli, come here."

I stepped down off the chair. My Howdah lay on the ground where I'd dropped it; my pistol was still in its holster. I moved to stand in front of him.

He gazed at me then commanded, "Strip naked, then turn slowly, Ms. Fatelli."

I did, and made a slow pirouette, letting him view everything as he'd demanded. The cold bit at me, making me shiver. It wasn't important. What was important was the next command. I could see the burning eyes of the other men as I turned, but what normally sent my hackles rising, did nothing now. Their leering gazes meant nothing. They did not exist for me. My entire being waited for my master's next command. The cold bit at me, making me shiver. It wasn't important. What was important was the next command.

It wasn't long in coming. Cameron gazed at me and, when I met his gaze, he turned it on Ginny and declared, "Take her back to the cabin you took her from, throw her in, then jump in the room yourself."

I walked over to Ginny and grabbed her by the arm, marching her away. We left the room and walked out into the now-strengthening blizzard. Ginny tugged at me a few times, but I maintained my grip as we walked to the lone cabin just north of all the others.

"Ms. Fatelli — Fern — you don't have to do this! We're not mindless slaves. You know that."

I knew it, but it didn't matter. It wasn't what mattered. The blizzard didn't matter. The biting, chilling cold didn't matter. Being naked didn't matter. What mattered was moving Ginny into the cabin, and jumping in after her.

She started struggling in earnest, throwing her forearm against my wrist holding her arm. I tightened my grip, and started pulling her towards the cabin faster. I wanted to finish my command. Ginny, obviously, had other ideas. She didn't want to go, but I made her — step by reluctant, fighting, step.

I'd managed to drag her through the blizzard to the cabin. My body shook uncontrollably, but I'd made it to the end. My mission would be a success once she was inside. Then a bomb burst behind my eyes.

Ginny was in my head. I could feel her there: pulling, tearing at something that I didn't want to let go of. It hurt so much. I was blinded, dropping to my knees in the fierce blizzard. Naked and shivering, it was only good fortune that had kept me alive to now.

Ginny held me close as I tried to see. She held on to me and whispered, "You're not controlled any more. I cut the magick threads. You aren't controlled by that thing. You don't have to do what he says anymore."

It was all I could do to keep from falling over. My head hurt, and I shivered so hard that I could barely stay up, even with Ginny supporting me.

"How did you do that?" My teeth chattered like castanets as I tried to form coherent words.

Ginny smiled, shivering, and began to help me walk. "Psychic, I guess. I can feel when something's off in a person, and it's like grabbing at greasy, spongy thread, and pulling it apart." She shrugged, or maybe shivered, and got my right arm across her shoulder. "It just works. I'm not affected by stuff like that. I guess I'm just immune to magick."

The information should have been portentous. To my semi-frozen brain, and nearly frozen body, warmth was all I was truly about. Warm equals survival. Simple equation … hard to meet when you're naked in below-freezing weather.

Ginny walked around the cabin to the side, getting out of the raging wind and blinding snow. "We have got to get you warm. Is there a place you know we can hide?"

Her concern for me blew away like the snow. I couldn't stop shivering. Ginny still had my arm over her shoulder. She started back towards the cluster of cabins, angling to our right, towards a dark cabin between two lit ones. Ginny was shivering as bad as I was when we finally stumbled inside.

Ginny managed to rip her cloth sack covering wide enough to barely cover us both. We pulled each other close, trying to warm up. Fortunately, being out of the howling wind helped, as did the closed space of the cabin. In there, our shivering had its intended effect, and we slowly warmed up to the point we could hold a conversation without our staccato teeth cutting each word.

"What now?"

Ginny stood at the lone window, peering out, watching for any movement. I was still wrapping my head around what Ginny had done to me … and for me. My head was no longer wrapped in that cottony euphoria of waiting for Cameron's slightest whim. No way was I going back to that.

"First, we get warm. I can cast a warming spell. Next, we have to get the others away from Cameron." I turned my gaze down, thinking. "Then, we have to help those babies."

I looked back up at Ginny, who flashed a bleak grin when she turned to me.

"All without getting caught, eh?" She gestured at the towers that Sinera had taken out earlier. "And without being seen. How is that going to work?"

Her voice quavered only a little bit. She was scared. So was I. Cameron would be expecting me to come back soon, I was certain. If I did, I was pretty certain he'd notice I was free of the compulsion.

That meant whatever we were going to do, we needed to do it as quickly as possible. I rested for a few minutes more, then reached for that underground power. It was there — like a ley line, but not. This was the first time I really paid attention to what I was pulling from. It was more like a reservoir of magick, like a deep well that provided water even in a drought.

I pulled at this source, and it answered with a current of power that rolled into me, setting my skin to tingling. The "warm me up" spell was trivial with this power. The magick eagerly shaped itself to my will.

There was no ritual needed to fulfill the design of the spell. I simply guided it by intent, not by construction. That had started after I'd been possessed by the dragon, Anolyn, who'd been killed by a contingent of Elves. Those Elves had wanted to make more glass bottles for Ahiah, the Nephilim. I wasn't certain how it all fit, but it was what the dragon had left me with when the battle with the Elf lord Cobb had finished.

I had a grasp on all this magick that I hadn't before. By osmosis, instant learning, or stolen knowledge — I had no clue. It just worked. As the warming spell took hold, and my shivering subsided, I was very happy that it'd happened.

Once I'd warmed up, I cast it on Ginny, using the drawn power to set it in place for the next twenty-four hours. Now warm, we needed to move. No matter how careful I was, I couldn't be sure if Cameron's pet wizards could track the magick disturbance. I worked a "Don't notice me" around Ginny and myself, then we walked back outside into the blizzard.

The flakes stung as they hit my bare skin. They melted instantly on the warming spell. So soon Ginny and I looked like we'd just stepped out of a shower, naked and trailing water. It would make us easy to follow, but I hoped the storm would cover our tracks before anyone came by.

"So, you're here to rescue me?" Ginny asked with a half-smile on her lips.

The snow eddied around us a moment, then resumed blowing.

"I'm out here to salvage my reputation. Which means rescuing you, yeah. You could put it that way."

Her smile faltered momentarily, then she turned her head. "So long as we live through it, I don't care the reasons."

"Yeah, my thoughts too."

We trudged close enough to the jumble of cabins to start to see their outlines through the blowing snow. We'd drifted a little north of the cluster. The "Don't notice me" was working fine: none of the watch tower crews raised an alarm as we trudged past them.

"Let's go back to the women's barracks and see if my clothes are there, and if we can find some for you. I'm not exactly wanting to flash my tits at everyone we walk by, even if they're not paying attention to us."

We kept our voices to soft whispers, because we weren't really invisible, just something that people wouldn't pay attention to unless their attention was drawn to us.

Ginny grumbled, "So what's the plan?"

I slogged through the calf-high snow as the blizzard swirled around us. "First, clothing. Second, find where everyone is. Third, figure it out from there."

Ginny nodded. "Good enough for now."

We made it back to the women's barracks, and stepped in through the hole where the door used to be. The inside swirled with chilling wind, making the opening sound like the groan of a tortured soul. Our clothes were in the corner where we'd thrown them when Cameron had ordered us to strip down.

There wasn't a set for Ginny, which was going to be a problem. I threw Dean's suit to her. She was close to his size, and the clothing would keep bullets out of her if we were discovered. She put it on, zipping it closed as I finished snapping the webbing into place around my waist. The knife was still there, as were the ammo reloaders for the snubnose. The guns were gone, confiscated by the cultists.

I wondered what they'd done with Fawn. Dean, JC, and Sinera were friends I cared about, but Fawn was my sister. She came first. She was also our best bet in getting out of this alive.

"Okay. Part Two: Find where Fawn and the others are."

# 26

WE STARTED OUT GOING EAST. Our intent was to make a slow loop around the camp. It took a bit, as there were groups of men in twos and threes walking throughout the place. Two men had checked the cabin I was supposed to throw Ginny into just moments after we'd left it. When they reported us being nowhere to be found, Cameron raised holy hell, pardon the pun, about it.

The patrols were out, and his pet wizards were sniffing everywhere for magick traces. One complained to his partner that finding us in this storm would be next to impossible: too much cold, too much wind, too much discomfort to concentrate. We found JC as we moved east to avoid the biggest cluster of searchers. He was on the far East side of the compound.

He'd been staked out, still naked, in the middle of the howling wind and snow. I know Orcs are supposed to be tough, but not even an Orc can handle staked out naked in a full-on blizzard for long. Two guards huddled miserably next to a vertical piece of plywood about three meters away from him. The pitiful windbreak kept the worst of the wind off of them, but it was still in the middle of the storm.

Despite them being crazed, bugnuts cultists, I sympathized a little. They had to be on Cameron's shit list to be here. That didn't excuse why they were there. They were there to make sure JC froze to death. That killed any concern for them.

I handed my small knife to Ginny. "Get the rope. I'll watch the watchers."

Ginny nodded, her eyes wide. She swallowed, then slowly moved forward, the soft crunch of snow lost in the swirling wind as she shifted behind JC's stake. I moved over to where the two men huddled. If there was going to be trouble, I could cut it off by being in the right place at the right time.

I carefully stepped closer to the flimsy windbreak. The two men had hunched their coats up over their ears as they watched JC shiver his life away three meters from their dubious shelter. Ginny worked at the ropes, quietly slicing through them as I stayed alert for any change in the two guards.

When the rope parted, JC dropped into a fetal position at the base of the stake, shivering uncontrollably. It took a moment for the guards to react.

"Hey, why'd he drop?" the one with the dark parka asked the other.

He was dark-skinned compared to his partner, who looked pale as the snowflakes swirled through air around them. He let his checked hunting jacket drop down to his shoulders.

"I dunno. Cover me while I check him out, eh?"

He leaned his rifle next to his friend, and stalked over to the huddled Orc.

He gave JC a vicious kick, then snarled, "Get up, tater. You ain't allowed to lay down!"

While JC had their attention, I grabbed the rifle and swung it just as the parka-clad man noticed the movement. He turned towards me and took the full force on the rifle of his face. He crumpled, moaning in pain, his hands covering his shattered features. The other man spun to face me. His eyes grew wide, frightened by my sudden appearance.

Suddenly, he lifted up on his toes. A harsh thud came from between his legs. He dropped to the snow-packed earth, moaning in pain, trying to curl around his screaming testicles.

Ginny glanced up at me, then gave a tight grin that looked more like a snarl.

"God, that felt good." She limped back towards JC, then turned her head. "Coming? Or are you going to let him freeze?"

I blinked the snow from my eyes, then trudged over to JC. The warming spell almost cast itself as I focused on the lean Orc. After a minute of shivering, JC warmed up enough to orient himself and stand. He was still naked. That was tremendously apparent when he straightened. Ginny blushed crimson and turned away. Me, well … it was impressive. I realized after a few moments that I had no clue if JC was still controlled or not.

"Ginny, can you check him the way you did me?"

She mumbled something, keeping her back to JC and shaking her head emphatically. Okay, now this went from cute to dangerous. If we had to argue about it, then we were just saying that the cultists could come find us right here. It was time to take control of the situation.

"Ginny, we don't have time to be embarrassed. Now check JC right now!" I snarled at her.

Her back stiffened and, for a moment I thought she was going to fight me out of sheer mulishness, but Ginny slowly walked to where JC's front wasn't so ... distracting, then stared at his head. JC grabbed his temples, nearly falling. I moved forward to help. Ginny jumped back with a little squeak of embarrassment.

JC steadied himself, then looked over at me, then down at himself. I didn't know Orcs could blush. He turned a darker shade of yellow green from head to toe and hunched over, covering his genitals with large hands.

"Uh, ma'am, can you find me some pants? I would like not to flash you for the next, uh, whenever we get out of here?"

That got a half-stifled giggle out of Ginny, whose ears remained crimson.

I smiled, self-consciously looking only at his eyes. "We'll see what we can do."

The trip back to the women's barracks was as nerve-wracking as it was when we set out looking for JC. Once we got there, JC scrambled back into his clothing with a happy sigh, getting one from Ginny also. This time, we took the other clothes with us. I didn't want to keep coming back here. We were taking enough chances as it was.

"So what next? I know Dean was tossed in a cabin. And Fawn's with that bastard Cameron. I didn't see what happened to Sinera."

That made Dean the next priority. If Cameron was keeping Fawn, he might have Sinera with him too. That being the case, he might not try to kill them. I really wanted to rush off after him, but Dean, naked and dumped in the cabin, had to be first. We knew where he was. We didn't know where Fawn and Sinera were.

Before we left, JC flipped over one of the few empty beds, then tore two of the metal legs off. "Throwing if I need to; clubs if I don't," he said as I looked at the destruction.

It made sense to me: get a weapon wherever you can.

I recast the "Don't notice me" spell, just to make sure it was working. Then we left the women's barracks and snuck carefully West, working slowly towards where JC said Dean was being held. There were no guards near the cabin. They probably were with the other teams spread out in the compound looking for us.

The cabin slowly appeared out of the swirling snow. It was the southern most of the last four cabins, closest to where we had snuck into the compound. I motioned JC and Ginny to move close to me. I lowered my voice so that the cultists that were passing us just at the edge of visibility wouldn't hear and break the spell.

"We're going to circle the cabin first," I murmured to them. "If Cameron's not a total idiot, there could be a trap on that cabin. He knows we're loose and, since Dean is supposed to be in here, it would be one place we'd come to."

JC raised an eyebrow.

"I do believe, Ms. Fatelli, that are you a touch paranoid," JC chuckled grimly. "Considering his wizards, paranoid is a proper caution." He gazed at the slowly disappearing knot of men and Troykin. "Wish I knew where that guitar case is. That little guy would be right handy about now."

I shuddered. That was one thing I really didn't want to find again. The one introduction had been enough to guarantee me some nightmares if we lived through this.

# 27

THE WIND WAS DYING as we circled the cabin from about three meters away. If there was any trap, I was guessing it'd be much closer to the cabin rather than randomly away from it. We didn't find any the hard way, so the next step was to get to the cabin, and avoid the most likely location for a trap. I believed if there was one, it'd be at the base of the wooden steps.

The snow didn't appear to have anything under it. The next most likely was a trap on the door, or a warding. I focused for a moment, then opened my mage Sight. The snow gleamed white as I looked around. The grays of the cabin and darker gray of the trees were stark in contrast to the snow. On the door I found an alarm warding.

It wouldn't shriek or blast us. It just alerted the caster that it had been disturbed. Simple, and effective. I didn't really know how to circumvent it without taking it down. The spell is simple. The caster sets the spell on a particular item he wants to ward, and the spell is tied to his own magick. If the spell is disturbed, it's like plucking a spider's web. The caster will know immediately that something's up.

So we were at a temporary impasse. I didn't know how to get around the ward, and tearing a wall down would get unwelcome attention. JC went around to the small window and peered in. "He's in there all right," JC said quietly. "On top of four other guys."

We walked around to the window. JC lifted me up to get a look. The stasis ward was still in place, meaning anyone going in would get hit by it and get themselves trapped there as part of the eventual ritual.

Another four men and a Troll trudged into view. The snow fell heavily now, the thick flakes descending vertically in the still air. I could see was maybe six meters ahead of me, at the most. We slowly kneeled down and stayed quiet until the group faded from sight in the falling snow.

"They're going to get lucky, or we're going to get careless eventually." JC stared in the direction the cultists had disappeared for several moments, then turned to Ginny and I. "As much as I would love to bounce their heads together, and go whoop-ass on this place, those casters and Cameron are nothing to mess with. I need my guitar."

Ginny looked at me, then stared at JC. "You want that killer thing loose in here?"

JC nodded. "Poetic justice. Besides, we'd stand a much better chance with Mack than without him."

"We don't need that thing. We need to get Dean loose, or find Fawn and Sinera. We don't, they're dead, and we'll be dead. So, what can we do here, right now?"

I was mad, and scared. The scathing comment caught both JC and Ginny by surprise. JC's mouth turned down, and he looked back again to where the last group of cultists had disappeared. Ginny looked anywhere but at me.

JC grunted as he turned to face me. "You're right. We need to do what we can. You have to understand though, that 'thing', as you put it, is a friend to me. So take a little care, please, about how you address him. His name's Mack."

I heard the tone in JC's voice. He was worried for the creature. I'd happily leave it for the ravens, if it was my choice.

What was the best choice? There were now four different priorities: Fawn, Sinera, Dean, and Mack ... the freaking guitar monster. Fawn came first to me. Dean was who we could help right now. The others had to come later. I hated the choice, but it was the only one to make.

"Can you make illusions, Ms. Fatelli?"

The question caught me by surprise. I'd never tried to, but if you thought about it, that was kind of what the "Don't notice me" could be thought of as: an illusion that we weren't worth noticing.

"Why? I don't think an illusion would exactly help us right now. Tyrannosaurs or Polar Bears don't exactly fit the terrain."

JC shook his head. "I meant the cabin. If you can make an illusion that the cabin is intact, I could punch through the wall closest to Dean, and we could maybe pull him free."

I hadn't thought of doing that.

"Let me test it first, and see if it works." I looked at Ginny. "Go out to where we were circling the cabin earlier, I think you'll still be in the radius of the 'Don't notice me'. I'll cast the spell and you can observe the results."

Ginny nodded and trudged out four meters and turned to face the cabin. I gathered my power, then began to envision a shell, with the face showing an undisturbed cabin that I could see in front of me. The magick flowed, eager to shape itself as I desired.

It was truly an odd feeling. Before I was possessed, magick was hard and slow for me. I had needed a ritual to pull the pieces together to make the spell I needed. Now, it was like I'd known magick in ways only the best practitioners knew. I could feel — and see, sort of — how the power settled around the cabin, hiding JC and I. I realized this much power is going to be noticed, so I focused on hiding its essence, which was surprisingly easy.

The next layer was hiding sound. The silence spell settled over the illusion, layering and blending with the original casting. It, too, was way too easy. I never had this kind of control, and it freaked me out. It still does. I feel like I've stolen something and the owner's going to come and take it all away. Anyways, the silence spell settled over the illusion, layering and blending with the original casting.

"Hit the wall, JC."

He grunted, then slapped his hand quietly against the wood. He didn't want to get attention if the spell didn't work. Ginny just stood there.

"Hit it again, a little harder."

JC complied, but Ginny didn't move. I walked out to Ginny, who suddenly oriented on me as I passed the edge of the spell.

"It's working! I didn't see or hear you until you walked out here!" she said in an excited, breathless whisper. She started to clap her hands, then stopped before she finished the move. "Guess I oughta not do that out here. Too many listening ears."

Ginny and I walked back inside the spell to watch JC rhythmically thumping the wall as he waited for us to come back.

"Looks like it's working just fine, ma'am," he said with a wide grin. He looked the wall over then shifted to the middle. He raised a meaty paw, then looked back at me. "Do we want to pull 'em all out, or just Dean?"

"Just Dean, JC. We don't know if the others are victims, or volunteers. Let's play it safe."

JC nodded, then punched the wall hard. The ground vibrated a bit as the cabin shuddered, taking the blow. The wood wall cracked, and JC struck it again, splintering the plywood exterior enough to get a hand grip. He pulled, and a large piece came free with a loud crack. Despite knowing the spell was up, we all stopped, listening for the cries of the cultists charging to get us.

When nothing happened after an hour-long minute, we slowly relaxed. JC grinned and tore at the wall. In a few minutes, he'd torn the plywood sheet off the side and we could see Dean on top of the other three men in the cabin.

JC made a loop out of his shoelaces, then used a piece of plywood to help push it around Dean's foot. I make it sound easier than it was. JC first tried to toss the loop over Dean's foot, but the loop wouldn't open. He then had Ginny hold the end of the shoelaces while he tried to toss it, but Ginny was too short, and JC's fingers were the size of Bratwursts, which made the tossing of a small object like the loop of shoelace problematic by hanging up on his fingers.

We were all growing a little nervous. No one had come by to check the door of our cabin, but that could happen. Dean then got the idea of putting the loop over a splintered piece of wood. It worked on the first try.

A steady, slow pull later, Dean rolled through the hole, falling in the snow.

He was up and moving in an eyeblink, shouting at the sudden cold.

"Jeebus! What the hell?!" Dean spun looking for attackers.

The noise should have had the cultists swarming all over us. Instead, there was just silence. Then he looked down at himself.

His eyes grew wider as he realized he was totally naked. He squawked like a startled chicken and his hands flew to cover himself.

I couldn't help it. I giggled. Dean's head came back up, and he glared at me. Then, a moment later, he began to chuckle ruefully.

"Here, I think this one'll fit you." I tossed Sinera's stealth suit to him. He wasted no time in pulling it on. Sinera was longer in the limbs, so he bunched the material up. It looked uncomfortable, but being warm trumped comfort. He was mildly disappointed to find that he had no ammo clips or knives.

"Could've used them, but I'll make do with what we got." He shrugged, much more relaxed now that he was covered up. "So what now? I've been sleeping while you all were doing some rescuing. What have I missed?"

"JC was staked out. You were tossed in a cabin. Ginny's with us. Fawn and Sinera are missing, but JC thinks they're with Cameron. Sneaking our way to him is our next step."

"I think our next step would be to get a few weapons …" Dean replied quietly. "We're screwed if all we bring is an empty fist to a gunfight, and lots of the fellas here have guns."

JC nodded. Ginny looked down, unwilling to get into the conversation. She'd seen a little more of Dean than she'd wanted to.

Dean's idea was sound. Pulling it off ended up being another matter. The snow had begun to lessen, which made visibility easier. Coupled with clearing skies, anything we did would be hard to cover up. The walls of the camp worked against us too.

Cameron's wizards were sniffing for any magick and, so far, I'd been able to hide my castings enough that they couldn't zero in on us. The downside was that Cameron was no idiot. He knew for a certainty that we were still inside the compound.

His teams of armed men and wizards worked back and forth across the inside of the compound, checking buildings and snowdrifts. We kept moving with the teams staying in the tracks they made in the snow to hide our own. This went on for what felt like hours. When the patrols had covered the entire compound four times and hadn't found us, Cameron switched to using a beating line. He lined up his men so that they were only a little ways apart, then had them walk forward, holding formation. It made going around them more difficult, but he didn't have the numbers to extend the line from wall-to-wall without leaving big gaps we could snake through.

I have to admit it was satisfying to see all this effort come up empty. We were doing half of our job; the other half was getting outside to warn the MaRS team. Dean was the best choice, but he really wasn't a caster. We had a way out, but, once he was outside the compound, my magick couldn't hide him. Cameron had people outside the compound, and the towers likely had people in them again, so an escape was stymied.

Which meant we had to change our tactics. We had to find a way to disrupt Cameron's followers enough that there'd be no organized resistance when the MaRS people showed. Which brought us around to Dean's plan: getting weapons and reducing numbers.

I didn't like it. Attacking a group made us too easy to pinpoint. I really couldn't see any other way, though.

Then Cameron changed tactics again. This time we couldn't just avoid him.

# 28

"HELLO OUT THERE!" Cameron shouted from somewhere amongst the ramshackle cabins. "I have Ms. Fatelli and your Elf friend, people! If you want them not to be shot, you'll come out now and surrender yourselves! I don't want to kill you! We can make a deal! Besides, I already know about the special unit from Halifax coming out here!

"Ms. Fatelli volunteered the information! You don't want needless deaths on your heads, do you? Surrender, and I won't have to kill anyone. You've got one minute to walk in! Otherwise, we'll be down one, with one to go!"

I gritted my teeth. JC growled low and dangerously. Dean stared ahead, his face a study in stone. Ginny looked at the three of us and tried to talk reason.

"He is going to kill us all anyways. You saw those cabins!" she whispered fiercely. "He's going to throw us all in them and then do whatever they've been prepped for! We can't go in! *I* can't go in! No way am I going to let him get away with this kind of …"

I raised my hand and pushed it over her mouth. Ginny gasped in surprise and slapped my hand away angrily.

"What the fuck did you do that for!?"

"Ginny, he can't control you. Right?"

The question caught her off-balance. She ducked her head away from JC and Dean, who stared at her.

"I told you he can't …" she answered slowly.

She really didn't want others to know. She'd done all this to hide her ability. Her parents tried to exploit it. That school was exactly the same way: only trying to use her. Now, Cameron was trying to use her because of that gift, too. No wonder she'd gotten so defensive about letting others know.

"Plan on blabbing to everyone, 'Pyrrha'?" she angrily hissed at me.

"Look, there may be a way to use that against him. If you aren't able to be controlled, can you keep him from affecting us if we surrender?" I stared straight into her eyes, trying to will her to listen. "Ginny, if you can keep us from being caught by that … that thing, whatever it is, we've got a chance at tak—"

"I can't." She said it with a flat finality. "I can only protect myself. I can't stop him from zapping you with that thing." She looked at me. "I can't help you. I can barely help myself."

Well, crap. That was what I didn't want to hear. The minute was almost up, and we had no options. I looked from face to face, hoping someone looked like they had an idea. They all returned my gaze, hoping I had the solution.

I took a deep breath. "All those in favor of surrendering, raise your hand."

For a moment I thought I was the only one that was going to do it, but then Dean raised his hand, then JC. Ginny kept her hand down, and gave us all a desperate glare.

"You know he's going to kill all of you! He'll control you all. He'll put you two back on the stakes until the cold kills you and you, Ms. Fern will be tossed in that baby farm barracks, to get raped whenever one of those sickos feels like it. He'll throw —"

"I get it!" I snarled back.

I hated that she was right. I hated that this was happening. I hated myself for being so stupid and trusting Cameron when my gut told me not to. *"I get it"* that I was bone-weary of the fighting.

Cameron held all the cards he needed with Fawn and Sinera in his control. I knew he was going to kill us, but that little bit of hope that said everything will be all right got me on my feet.

I took a deep breath, and dismissed the "Don't notice me". The three cultists about jumped out of their skins when we appeared directly in front of them. They recovered quickly, though, and aimed their rifles at us.

"No funny stuff, eh? I don't want to shoot you, but I will if you try anything."

I nodded, as did Dean and JC. Ginny just hugged herself, rubbing her hands up and down her arms as tears tracked down her cheeks. Her shoulders slumped. She looked like the lost, frightened teenager she was. The three cultists marched us over to Cameron, and took positions near him.

Cameron smiled just like a smarmy televangelist. He had three men to his left in parkas holding shotguns. Sinera was there, naked and glowing with a heating spell. Fawn was there, too. Her naked body glowed like Sinera's. Both were armed: Sinera with her bandoleer of throwing knives, and Fawn with her FN-FAL.

Cameron walked towards us. The urge to break and run away was almost overwhelming. A shudder ran through me as I knew he was going to use that thing on all of us once more. I didn't ever want to be controlled like that ever again. Dying was beginning to look like the only option left.

Cameron stopped a few meters in front of us, still smiling like he was addressing a congregation.

"I am so glad to see you all, especially you, Ginny. You don't know how worried I have been about your welfare."

He stepped closer to Ginny, who shrank away from him, stumbling back into one of our captors. He chuckled viciously, and pushed her back at Cameron, who caught her, holding her upright when she wanted to collapse.

I can bet you're wondering, "Why didn't Fern jump him like an action hero? Everyone was distracted. You had the upper hand with dean and JC with you."

It wasn't that easy. Cameron has three friends with him. I didn't know how many of the guard towers had guns trained on us, and I knew that someone was going to get shot if anything started. There were just too many ways to get killed.

It's like a victim, knowing they're going to be killed, will walk quietly with their killers, trying to extend their life one instant longer. Or, a victim whose given up entirely. They're so lost in the control of their killers that they lose all will to resist, and become sheep to be slaughtered.

I hate admitting it, but that's what happened to me. I couldn't think of a way out, and the despair had started to overwhelm me. I'd been through that heart-deadening despair once already. Maybe that's what made it easier to fight off this time. It really wasn't fighting so much as not wanting to lose control again.

"Hey! You gonna get past the cheesy villain monologue? Or are we going to have to listen to it all again, 'cause last time I wanted to puke, and I know my stomach couldn't take it a second time!"

Cameron's jaw dropped open, as did a few of the guards. JC and Dean chuckled, which was a bad thing for them.

Two very unhappy loyal followers used the butt ends of their weapons to knock both the Orc and man to the ground, and then to commence kicking them viciously. The nastiest was a Troykin who'd taken JC's bed leg clubs from him, and proceeded to beat him across his back with them. Their jagged ends tore his suit apart and, after a half-minute of maniacal beating, his back started to resemble hamburger. Cameron lifted his hand, and the cultists backed off.

Dean lay face-down in the snow, not moving. Blood spattered the snow around JC from his beating, but he was still conscious. He coughed, then pushed himself onto his hands and knees.

Cameron motioned at Fawn and Sinera, who stepped forward. "Take him over to that cabin and throw him in."

They jumped to it, eager to do his bidding.

He turned to us then shouted, "RELEASE!", just as he had in the barracks.

This time I could feel the shift from terror to … love. A very small part of my mind registered the change, but it just didn't matter. I waited patiently to hear what he was going to tell me.

"Ms. Fatelli," Cameron said, addressing Fawn, "Please take your sister Fern to Cabin CH, and throw her in. She'll make a good addition there." Cameron looked over at me. "Get up, Ms. Fatelli, and walk with your sister Fawn to the cabin."

I got up, and fell in step beside Fawn. That it was three of my steps to her two didn't matter. I had been given an order, and my mind sang with the joy of being useful. But the niggling buzzing at the back of my head wouldn't completely go away.

As we walked off, I heard Cameron order three of the cultists to take Ginny to cabin 'H'. Because the order wasn't directed at me, it was easy to ignore. Fawn and I moved into the dense cluster of cabins, then turned right past the women's barracks. She led me between four cabins, to one that was partly isolated just west of the cluster. 'CH' marked the edge of the roof overhang.

Fawn grabbed me and the little buzzing exploded in my skull.

# 29

F AWN AND I BOTH DROPPED TO THE GROUND, clutching at each other as Cameron's beguilement was torn to shreds by the wild magick within us. I gasped, pulling a lungful of air to scream just as Fawn's hand clamped over my mouth.

"Shhh! He thinks you're tossed in the cabin. I'm going to stand here until he orders me to move. Do that spell you did before and hide yourself. I don't think he's going to come check to see if I threw you in."

I nodded, still breathing hard. I wanted to run as far away, as fast as I could. It was a small miracle that none of the guard towers had noticed us and raised an alarm. *Why hadn't they?*

I thought for a moment. If Cameron's power was so encompassing, maybe they'd been told to look for the MaRS team and weren't paying attention to anything else. Thinking about my own experience, that was a big hole in Cameron's power. Not that it would help anyone held by it, but knowing that his commands were literal was an advantage.

I never did anything beyond the command I was given by Cameron when I was held before, so it's possible that the others that Cameron controlled worked the same way. Either that, or the cultists were as dense as a rock.

A literal command was easy to take advantage of. Dumb and stupid is a lot tougher, because dumb and stupid are so creative in their idiocy. I really hoped I was right about that.

Fawn grabbed me by the shoulder. As she did, the buzzing started again. Fawn gasped and let go.

"What the hell?"

"Don't ask me. Whatever it is happened ... happened twice now. The first time ..."

"I know the first time. What I want to know is why it's happening." She stared at me, then turned to gaze in the direction we'd come from. "We need to figure this out. Something is really off in a bad way right now. I really don't want more of the same in my life."

I agreed with Fawn on that. There was too much weirdness going on for either of us to be remotely comfortable. What we needed were answers. Fawn kept her eyes scanning the direction we came from.

"Get that spell done, Fern. I think I see movement between the cabins."

I didn't wait. I concentrated like I had earlier. The power from my sister was amazing. She was like some big battery that never lost a charge. Between her, and that magick source below the ground, the compound was an enormous wellspring for power. That force roared into me, and shaped itself to my will.

I got the "Don't notice me" up just as a group of four men walked out from between the cabins and moved towards Fawn.

I used a few precious moments to focus on hiding the magick signature.

I hoped the other wizards didn't notice the surge when I set the spell up. I stepped to Fawn's left as she stared at the cabin, making sure no one would bump into me by accident.

Two of the men stopped a couple meters away. The man with the blue-and-black checkered hunting jacket carried an assault rifle; the one in the green camo military coat held a hunting rifle. The other two, one in a leather coat, and the other in a white coat with a red maple leaf on the left breast, moved to flank Fawn.

"You're supposed to come with us. The Reverend is waiting for you," the one in the white coat said.

They waited for a moment as Fawn continued to stare at the cabin.

The other man sighed. "She ain't gonna move unless Cameron comes to get her. She just listens for him."

The man waved his hand in front of Fawn's face, then slapped her butt. Fawn didn't flinch. I had to clench my teeth hard to keep from shooting them. The two men chuckled.

"See? We aren't important. The Reverend is what she is listening for."

The man in the leather coat nodded, then his chuckle took on a more ominous tone. "Heh, I wonder just how much she'd let us do while she waited." He looked over at White Parka. "What do you think?"

The guy in the white parka shook his head.

"I think if you try that, you might have a real problem with her. Listening or not, I'll bet you that you try to 'have fun' with her, you'll get torn to shreds." He smiled and added, "Don't forget, she took on Chuck hand to hand and beat him. I haven't ever heard of a girl beating a Troll like a dirty rug, have you?"

That got through to Leather Coat, and he backed away from Fawn, then turned towards the cabins. White Parka fell in step with the red-and-black checked hunter and the one in camo, and trudged towards the cabins to report to Cameron.

I followed them back. Cameron still had Sinera next to him, along with his cadre of three wizards. I remembered there being four, and wondered if the missing one was doing searches with the cultists, or had gotten hurt somehow.

Cameron was talking to the wizards as I approached. "Make certain that you each get your circles cleaned off and ready for tonight. We've got everything in place." He turned to the four men. "Where's the blonde? You were supposed to bring her back."

The four men looked at each other. The one in white shuffled his foot as he replied, "She didn't listen to us. She just kept staring at nothing. Wouldn't move for Steve; wouldn't move for me neither. She was like a zombie, just waiting for you to say something."

Cameron stared at the man with undisguised contempt. "So I have to figure out how to do everything now? Go back, and bring her here. Carry her if you have to."

He turned abruptly back to the three wizards, dismissing the four cultists, who sullenly turned back towards where they'd left Fawn.

So, now I had a choice to make. One, go back and warn Fawn, then take out the four guys. Fawn could do it by herself, but with all of them carrying guns, someone would get a shot off, and then we'd be back where we were before. Two, see about freeing Sinera, and then taking Cameron before he could take us. I didn't see that as a good option either.

I made the hard choice, and went for Sinera. More than anything, I wanted to go to my sister, but Sinera was here and close. If I could find a way to free her, we could surprise Cameron. That was my idea ... before the MaRS team surprised everyone and blew the front gate open.

# 30

T HE BLAST THREW PIECES OF THE GATE FAR AND WIDE. The MaRS team came pouring through where it had been. A few men tried to resist, but MaRS members shot them down before they had the chance. I moved to Sinera and grabbed her arm, willing power into her. It worked when Fawn and I touched, maybe it would here.

It turned out to be a bad idea, as Sinera drew two of her knives and slashed at my hand. Only through a lot of luck did she miss — and not by much. She reoriented and struck out again, by which time I'd scrambled far enough back to avoid the attack. I lost control of the "Don't notice me" and Sinera half-turned, looking down at me. She surged forward, and all I could think to do was to cover up in hopes she wouldn't hit anything vital.

I must have projected something like a wall, because there was a thud and, when I looked up, Sinera was staring back, rubbing a trickle of blood from her nose as she tried to discern the extent of the wall in front of her. She walked counter-clockwise, scuffing snow at me, only to see it stop short and slide off the invisible wall.

She kept circling like a starving wolf looking for an opening to kill its prey. I turned in place, keeping her to my front. I slowly stood up. Sinera tried to rush me, then stopped short of impacting the wall. She raised her voice. The liquid cadence of Elvish formed a glowing ball that moved to my makeshift wall. The sphere of magick flattened on my wall, flowed along it, then severed my connection to it. The spell collapsed.

Sinera charged. I threw myself sideways in a vain attempt to avoid being stabbed. Sinera hit me and we went down in a tumbling mass of arms, legs, and weapons. Sinera shifted liquid-quick, stopping our movement with a braced leg. She was on top, hand on my chest, holding me flat on the ground. The other hand lifted a knife high. I knew it was going to get me. I couldn't get out of the way. I was going to die. Suddenly, as the knife descended, a bullet hit Sinera in the thigh, knocking her to the ground.

I rolled on top of her, placed my hands on her temples, and summoned power. The reservoir below us answered and the power roared into me and, through me, into Sinera.

Her back arched as if she was being electrocuted. As the power built, I got faint glimpses of things that looked like moving black spots on a white background. Black spots becoming red spots. A sense of purpose — of focus. Sinera screamed as the power made her body vibrate. I could feel the spell strain, then snap, and I willed the power back to me.

It didn't want to come back, and threatened to draw me with it back into the maelstrom of Sinera's drowning mind. In desperation, I pulled at it. Instinct made me hold my hand up as I willed the power out and into the air. The air ionized, turning golden as the power punched up into the clouds. My body locked up like I'd grabbed a live wire. I arched helplessly. Every cell in my body burned; I felt as if I was being dipped in acid.

The power finally faded, leaving me an aching mess. Sinera groaned, rolling to her side and curling in a fetal position from the pain. I mirrored her. Below us, something shifted, like a leviathan of magick rolling over in a restless sleep.

Two men in grey urban camo jumpsuits ran to us. The stockier of the two grabbed Sinera in a shoulder carry. His partner, his hair sticking out from under the balaclava looked red. He grabbed me and carried me towards the blown gate.

"ALL OF YOU LOOK AT ME!" Cameron's voice roared above the gunfire.

People turned, and stopped moving.

"YOU WILL LINE UP AND —"

He never finished the sentence. A loud bang cut him off mid-sentence. I didn't see what happened, but I saw Cameron fall over, falling face down in the snow as four MaRS members cautiously moved in to surround him.

The last I saw of the action was Fawn stalking towards the prone Cameron, then we were through the blasted gates. The MaRS members carrying me and Sinera double-timed it towards a pair of black vans to their right. They deposited us back on the ground and a MaRS member with Emergency Medical Training flashed a light in our eyes to check for a concussion or drug reaction.

Satisfied that he found neither, he had us sit on the back bumper of the other van while he covered Sinera's naked body with a blanket. He draped one over my shoulders, then started prepping his gear for more arrivals. Sinera shivered, clutching the makeshift robe tighter around her body. She wouldn't look me in the eyes; she just stared at the ground.

"Hey, it's all okay," I told her. "We're out, and Cameron's little nuthouse is shut down. All we have to do is wait for Fawn, JC, and Dean to show up, and we can get the heck back to Dayning and sleep in some warm, comfortable beds."

Sinera shivered, and pulled at the blanket again. Her eyes were haunted. I'd never seen an Elf so shaken up before. The mental image of them being made out of animate marble shattered as I watched her try to pull herself together. She opened her mouth, then closed it, still staring at the snow-covered earth. Then, almost imperceptibly, she began to rock back and forth.

The rocking grew stronger as her teeth clenched and her eyes widened. Every exhale through her clenched teeth sounded like a faint baby's cry. The sense of pain had me seeing the wooden cage, and Cobb, walking out the door with Kent over his shoulder. Kent's head tilted up and gave me a despairing smile as he was taken from the room to be tortured to death for no reason I could understand.

I shook my head and shivered. That was going to haunt me for sure tonight. The pain, and the screams, had woken too many raw wounds.

A rising whine from Sinera jolted me back to the present. She was losing it. How do you get an Elf to stop letting her mind run wild? With Humans, sometimes a slap will shock them into focus, but I remembered the bandoleer of blades Sinera carried. I prefer my skin unventilated.

As I struggled with what to do, Sinera opened her mouth and screamed loud and long. The EMT jumped her in an eyeblink, jabbed a needle in her arm through the blanket, and depressed the plunger. Sinera gasped and turned on the EMT, her blades coming out, one in each hand.

Fear had me tackling her from behind, and we both fell in a shrieking, struggling heap at the back of the MaRS van. The drug acted fast, and her thrashing stilled. The EMT had me help him lift her into the back of the van.

"Damn, I thought she was going to gut me for sure. Thanks."

I nodded, and sat back down, my body shaking from the adrenalin dump. Two EMT's came running out with a MaRS member in between them. The EMT jumped out of the back and sprinted to them, checking the man over as they stagger-ran to the back of the van, rolling the man onto his back next to the unconscious Sinera.

# 31

T HE EMT WENT TO WORK IMMEDIATELY, unbuckling the chest plate and opening the man's shirt to expose a long groove on the side of his neck from which blood pulsed freely.

"Sh-shit. I think the jugular's nicked. Either of you a caster?"

The men shook their heads. The EMT grumbled and placed his hands over the blood and began a quiet chant. The two MaRS members stepped past the EMT and picked up Sinera, moving her further back in the van to clear room.

"Oh crap! What's happened?!"

I nearly jumped out of my skin. As it was, I startled hard enough that I fell backwards and landed on my butt in the snow.

Fawn helped me up.

"You're the one with the EMT training. I'd do it but I have to go back and coordinate the search."

She didn't wait for an answer, and loped off back into the compound. I looked over at the EMT who was holding his hand out.

"You got the training, you know what's going to happen. Beggars can't be choosers. Jugular's been nicked. I need a volunteer to pull from. You're it."

I swallowed and nodded, shifting next to the EMT.

"This is going to hurt, miss. There's a mouth guard in my bag."

He shifted to his left, his knees by the wounded man's ears, making room for me to kneel next to him.

"Just do it."

I gritted my teeth, and grabbed his hand. The EMT didn't look at me. He held his attention on the wounded man. I could feel a slight pressure of magick. The pull would have been ferocious and painful if I hadn't had all this weirdness. Instead of feeling a raw, burning claw inside my chest, it felt more like an insistent itch, like when I had poison ivy as a kid.

The pull faded, and the EMT released my hand. He was dripping with sweat as he removed his hand from the man's neck. I saw a smear of blood, but no bullet furrow and, most importantly, no leaking blood. He'd healed the wound completely.

"Man, that's the most I've ever drawn from someone at once." He took a shaky breath, sitting down between Sinera and the MaRS officer. "I am so glad I don't have to do that every day."

I knew I should feel totally drained. But I was ready to do it again … and again, if it was needed. There was a loss of magick, sure, but nothing more than what you might use to light a fire or make a glowing light. Yes, it takes magick, but not a large amount. It made me wonder where it all came from. Me? Obviously. But how did little young me get a reservoir of magick that big?

I mean, it's obvious I pulled a lot from that reservoir in the ground, but it was all used when Fawn and I did our casting. There shouldn't be that much left.

Larry did tell us, back when we'd survived our encounter with Ahiah, that we were batteries. I'd listened, then dismissed it, as everyone is a magick battery, really. The only difference is set by a person's own affinity, ability to control magick, and practice. I made a note to ask Larry to explain himself a lot more the next time I saw him.

Right now, I was both elated and confused by this power. Uncle Todd had said they'd walled off something when he'd pulled Fawn and I off our parent's casting circle when we were kids. They were trying to save us from being killed by a disease, and had bargained with a ... something that promised it would save us both, if they killed us on the casting circle. Uncle Todd couldn't stop our parents from doing the casting, and he didn't kill us like he was supposed to.

The casting went crazy. Uncle Todd took us back home, where he and Aunt Ruthie had cast a circle to stop some kind of black mist ... smoke stuff from flowing into us. Uncle Todd thought their spell on Fawn and I stopped whatever was happening to us. When our folks were declared dead by "magick misadventure", Uncle Todd and Aunt Ruthie stepped up as our new parents, and raised us as their own.

It'd been years since we lived with them. Aunt Ruthie had died eight years ago; Uncle Todd four months ago. All this craziness since we crossed paths with Hervald Thensome and that glass bottle.

I was so lost in my head with all this I didn't react at first to the screams from inside the compound. I jumped out of the back of the van and ran towards the screams, which gives you some idea of my lack of survival instinct. Truthfully, though, I was terrified that the screams were Fawn's. That was what propelled me back into that place.

I ran in through the splintered gate, looking for the source of the screams, and found it right in front of me. Some cabins, the ones we'd found those catatonic bodies in, had begun to sink. Worse, they glowed with magick. A couple of the nearby cabins had their doors open. One had two MaRS team members fully inside, collapsed on the pile of bodies. The other contained a very still MaRs member partway in. As I watched, two other MaRS team members pulled her free from the spell inside the cabin.

The cabins were sinking. Magick shrouded each one like a silk cocoon. The structures groaned as they were pulled down, slowly, but inexorably. The ground actually rose to envelop the structures.

I spotted Fawn to my left, and I sprinted over to her. We watched as the cabin sunk to the lower edge of the one window.

"Dammit! What can we do?! Think girl! Get your head into this situation and think!" Fawn berated herself, and I would have too, if I had her job.

You're watching people you lead and care about die, and there's nothing you can do, except commit suicide by trying to pull them out.

There had to be a way. But for the life of me I couldn't see it. Fawn screamed in frustration, then the reservoir shifted again. As it did, the cabins sank another half-meter down.

Fawn looked over at me. "You think the magick reservoir and the sinking houses are connected?"

# 32

F AWN STARED AT ME LIKE I HAD THE ANSWER. I didn't. But we both could sense it. That had to mean something in all this. Everything has a reason. Fawn drilled that into me when she practiced for the police academy. Everything happens for a reason. If you understand the reason, then you can begin to understand what motivates the criminal. Maybe that would work here.

I was surprised at my own thoughts. Here I was, with no special magick training, believing that I could actually logic out what was happening with a ley line. Yeah, and cabins weren't supposed to sink into the ground, either. Whatever was going on, it had to do with magick. Maybe we could check to see if something shifted to cause this disaster.

I was about to reach for Fawn's hand when she said, "Fern, grab my hand, and let's see if something's changed in that … thing down there."

Sisters, we think the same.

"Okay."

That's me, Ms. Decisive. It wasn't hard to say "yes". When you're desperate, anything sounds like a good idea.

I grasped Fawn's hand, closed my eyes, and did my best to ignore the screams around me. Instead of drawing, this time we tried to pull ourselves down to the … well … whatever it was.

It was a roller-coaster ride. It was like being sucked inside out. My body vibrated and lashed sideways like a whip being cracked. I could see the small of my back, and the bottom of my feet. Then everything snapped back into place. We were … I really don't know how to describe it … hovering. That's the closest description I've got. We … "hovered" near the source of power.

It was like experiencing Nietzsche. We hovered in the Abyss, and it looked back at us. The sense of waiting was just creepy.

*Time?*

Both Fawn and I gasped. The word rolled over us like ice water. We didn't know what to say — or think. The raw power contained in that simple question was just overwhelming.

*TIME?*

Fawn managed to say, "Why?" as … it … repeated itself to us.

*Why? Why, time?*

There was a very powerful sense of confusion as it replied. What was certain beyond all doubt now was that this ley line — as I had been calling it — was nothing of the sort. It was alive! Alive and curious. And intelligent. And overwhelmingly powerful. It was made of magick. Fawn and I had been greedily pulling power from it, and now it was aware. Aware of us.

"Yes. Why, time?"

*Kill.*

I think it was the matter-of-fact way that one word sounded that made my heart rate go crazy. This thing … creature — whatever it was — was going to kill. Fawn blurted, or thought — I'm not sure which — the question out before I could.

"Kill what?"

*Everything.*

The immensity of the statement made it sound ludicrous. Like some crazy movie villain that planned to destroy the world. It didn't make any sense at all. At the same time, that it would say the word made me shiver.

I swallowed dryly. Fawn's hand gripped mine tighter. I looked over and up at her. Her lips were pulled back into a frightened snarl, and I could see her self winding up to fight.

This was not the time to start anything. It would squash us like bugs and not care. The only reason I could think that it even talked to us was that we had the gall to actually question it. That, or it was toying with us. The confusion when Fawn asked its question, though, shot that paranoid idea down. So I went with curious.

"Fawn, let me ask something."

She looked down at me, then noticed how tightly she was gripping my hand and loosened her death-grip. She nodded. The small break in her concentration kept the "fight or flight" under control for her.

Me, I couldn't figure why I was so calm. I guess it was just the fact that I knew I was dead if it decided it didn't like us for any reason, and I just shut all the emotion off.

I kind of understood now why Kent had smiled like he did when Cobb took him away to torture him to death. He had nothing left, and accepted what might come. He gave up. I hadn't given up, but part of me knew, with absolute certainty, that I had no chance at all to survive if it attacked. Suddenly, that "everything" was a lot more personal.

"Why kill everything?"

*Must. Time?*

It shifted and I heard muffled screams as the cabins sunk further into the ground

"No." Fawn spoke up with a desperate authority.

*Not time?*

The screams still battered my ears, and yet there was less ... terror in them. More a sense of concern, and coordination. That all changed when the cabins were pulled further into the ground. Now only the rooftops were above the surface. I could see it, but also feel it, as the thing below somehow formed a line of power to the cabins, and pulled.

*Hungry.*

"Stop!"

I don't know if that was Fawn or me who shouted. The word just was there. It caused the thing to stop.

*Hungry.*

It sounded petulant, almost like a child being told it couldn't eat until everyone was seated at the dinner table. The entity hadn't pulled at the cabins again. The sensation of hunger was in the magick. The cabins were where the food was. The magick of the creature rose towards the partly-engulfed buildings.

It couldn't be coincidence that the cabins were right over the entity. Sacrifices. That's what they were. For this thing. With all the magick it had, why would it need sacrifices? Why so many? Why were they piled up in certain cabins? Why were the cabins placed so oddly?

"Why are you doing this!?" Fawn was shouting.

I heard, dimly, other responding shouts that sounded far off in the distance. The longer we held hands, the less real things were becoming. It was like we were not really standing in the snow; we were just occupying the space where we should be standing in the snow, but we weren't really there. We were with it … the entity … thing … whatever.

*Must.*

"Why in all of the weird magick world do things underground always talk in single words?!"

Yeah, that was me. Mouth ahead of brain. It's gotten me in more trouble than the habit is worth. The last thing I expected was an answer.

*Hard.*

*To.*

*Commune. With. You.*

"It speaks! Well, Glory and Hallelujah, isn't that a keen surprise!"

The whole of the universe began to shake around us. The faint cries of surprise and fear made me realize that the ground *was* shaking. Our bodies stumbled as the ground rippled like a pond that'd had a brick thrown into it. People fell or scrambled to keep their balance. The cabins groaned at the abuse, a few splintering from the pressure. All around were the screams of fear and pain.

*You. Anger. Me.*

# 33

I T WAS WAKING UP. I'd pissed it off and now its anger was centering its attention on us.

"Fern, can't you just shut up?"

Fawn's voice through gritted teeth had its desired effect and I clamped my mouth closed. I wanted to scream, but knew it would just make things worse. Some perverse part of me wanted to, though. I didn't like this thing at all, and I'm pretty sure the feeling was becoming mutual.

Fawn asked the next question. "Why must you do this?"

*Hungry.*

"Oh for —! Just shut up with the 'hungry' crap!"

Despite my good intention, and we know where that leads you, I'd hit my silence limit. I was so sure we were going to die, I told myself I just didn't care anymore. I was thinking that it would be nice not to dream, to not watch my friends die over and over.

I screamed at it, "You whiny little piece of crap! I'll just … just …!" and ran out of steam.

Just so you know, leaving a sentence hanging like that is surprisingly effective at confusing things. Its attention was fixed on us now, with all its implacable ire. In desperation, I pulled at the magick that made up the entity for all I was worth. If I was going to die — and it really looked like it — I wouldn't go down without a futile attempt to live.

Fawn gasped as the power flowed into her from me. I couldn't gasp. My lungs froze with the huge river of power that roared into me from the thing. It was intoxicating. I pulled … and pulled, reaching for all the power I could. It flowed into me, filling me, yet leaving me hungrier than ever for more. Fawn screamed both in pain and ecstasy as the power filled us, expanding us past our physical limits.

It was a feedback loop. The more we took, the more we hungered. The more we filled the growing hunger, the more powerful we became. The more powerful we became, the more we took, and the more the hunger grew.

As the power filled us, our hunger grew, and other sources of power began to appear: many small dots of power above us, waiting to be absorbed. Each had just a limited amount of readily usable power, but the core! The Core! It glowed like the sun. Each core had power to fill my hunger — *our* hunger.

We started to reach for them, but there was something … a shell, in the way. Magick bound those cores to the shell … *cabin*. The description came weakly from some inner part of us. The cabin was an annoyance. The magick was a greater annoyance. It held what we hungered for, and held it out of reach. We couldn't take those savory bits without absorbing the magick around them. Our bottomless hunger made us want to do so.

The small part of me, and of Fawn, didn't want that. We wanted to stop. It was hard to struggle free, and so easy to listen to the siren call of power — power to shape what we wanted, how we wanted. Magick enough to make our desires reality. Magick enough to drown in.

That was the thought that tipped the scales. We'd been so ready to jump in, that neither of us even considered that pulling from an entity made of magick would also pull the entity's personality inside us. Now, it was here in us, influencing us with its very being. Hunger for anything that had magick; anger at anything that refused to be consumed. And tired ... tired enough to sleep forever without more magick.

Fawn and I had the same revelation. Still clasping each other's hand, we concentrated and focused on pulling as much from the creature ... being, whatever it was, as hard as we could. We couldn't hold any more magick, so it had to go somewhere.

While our spiritual bodies were underground with the creature, our physical ones remained above ground. We could see the near-buried cabins. With just a flick of magick, we pushed them back above ground. Our physical bodies absorbed the magick excess, and then shot it skyward, to dissipate in the atmosphere.

The being fought us, but we'd gotten hooked into its magick essence like ticks. And, like ticks, we drank its magick like blood, greedy for more. It thrashed, and fought to dislodge us, but with the two of us focusing together, we were too stubborn to be dislodged.

The magick burst upwards like a fountain of light and darkness and blood. Faint cries of horror and growls of hunger echoed in the ears of our physical bodies. The magick was affecting the people.

Everyone up there was suddenly ravenously hungry. We could feel it through the magick, just like it had affected us. The difference was: none of them had a sister to help hold them together. Nor did they have the strength to stop the magick from influencing them. Everyone — literally *everyone* — were suddenly eyeing each other like steaks set in front of a starving dog.

The creature bucked and thrashed, still trying to dislodge us. We had hit a wall. If we didn't drain the creature, it might well turn on us and do its level best to kill everyone here. If we kept draining it, and throwing the magick into the air, we were certain that everyone here would go crazy and try to eat each other. It was the classic "between the devil and the deep blue sea" — between a huge magick entity and a whole lot of ravenous cannibals.

You'd think there was a third option. There was, but it was desperation — which always seems like a good idea when you think about it, but time often says it's worse than you could have imagined. We could put the magick in the ground: into the very rock and earth we stood on.

With no other choice we could think of, thought turned to action. We concentrated, forcing the magick into the granite below. Both Fawn and I gasped with effort. Our bodies labored, that is; our spirits were underground with the thing below.

As more and more power flowed into the ground, the more the released magick joined the stream of it flowing into the ground. Like calls to like, I guess. All the magick came from the same entity, after all.

Said entity thrashed less and less as we kept pulling. The hunger continued to batter us, but that same hunger reinforced our focus. We used its own hunger against it, pouring its entire essence into the ground below the compound in one huge magickal grounding. It faded to a tiny spark of magick and consciousness. We kept trying to pull more, but there was nothing more to take. The entity, the last magick dregs of it, lay unmoving like a corpse in the ground. There was no sense of intelligence when we tried to contact it. There was no reaction to pulling at it. It was for all intent, and purpose, dead.

The ground within the compound was saturated with the entity's magick — a ravenous, desperate magick. We'd manage to re-direct that magick, only to curse the ground. The thing, whatever it was, would start reabsorbing its essence when we quit scattering it. How long would it take the being to pull all of the magick back together was something neither of us knew. We both hoped that it would take a very, very long time.

We rose slowly through the rock and earth to join with our flesh once again. When the merging completed, Fawn doubled over in pain.

"The baby", she gasped out, then began screaming.

I started screaming with her. Four MaRS members charged up and formed a double fireman carry, hustling Fawn to the EMT station. A short while later, the siren began wailing as the vehicle tore down the greasy trail towards the nearest hospital.

# 34

THE ADRENALIN SPIKE launched me into the PT Cruiser. I slammed the door closed while simultaneously starting the engine. Just as Dean got to the car, I yelled for him to get Ginny out of the cabin, and have everyone get a ride back to Halifax with the MaRS team. I didn't wait to check if he'd heard me or not. I pushed the PT Cruiser past any safe driving limit for the weather and road conditions, and tried to catch the EMT truck.

I could feel my sister ahead of me. The more we connected with each other by drawing magick, the more a link seemed to strengthen between us. Right at that moment, I knew roughly how far she was in front of me, how fast she was traveling and, how precarious her life — and the baby's — were. I was sick with fear when I finally caught up with them at Kiptu General Hospital in Dartmouth.

Fawn had been rolled immediately into ICU. I got there barely three minutes later. I didn't bother to park. I just exited the car and ran into the Emergency entrance, where a burly orderly stepped away from the check-in desk and stood, blocking my way.

"Miss, you're going to have to stay here. No one's allowed back in emer—"

"My sister's back there! She's pregna—"

The orderly got this bored look on his face that said he'd seen this kind of acting out before. He gave me a bland smile then reached towards me.

"I'm certain the doctors will do their best for your sister, miss, now if …"

His hand touched my shoulder with a solicitous confidence, which fueled my anger. I slapped his hand off my shoulder as the nurse stepped through the door from the check-in cubbyhole. He took a step towards me, determined to "escort" me to the waiting room lobby.

"Please ma'am, you need to clear the Emergency floor. Patients come —"

"I don't give a rat's squeaky little ass that you want me out of here, I'm going to see my sister, you lard-belly walking meat sack pimple on a goat's butt freaking —"

"Ma'am!" The nurse approached me with alarm and outrage, fighting for dominance on her features. "You need to calm —"

That just made it more unbearable. Fawn was fighting for her life, and I NEEDED to see her.

"I do not 'need' to do anything!", I shouted furiously. "I'm going to see my sister, and you're going to clear out and let me go see her, you retar—"

I was cut off in mid-rant by a polite cough behind me. I spun and came face to chest with a RCMP officer. My eye level was even with his badge, which had the number nine-seven-five-five, and his name, "Ferguson", just above it.

Officer Ferguson smiled humorlessly at me, then said in a quiet, controlled voice, "Ma'am, I understand you're distraught. But right now they're doing their best to help you."

He raised a hand as I gathered a lungful of air to bitch him out. "I'm going to give you a choice," he said in that quiet, solid voice. "You can listen to these fine emergency personnel, and wait in the lobby. Or, I can help you evacuate the emergency room, and I can take you to my precinct to wait in the drunk tank, with about ten others who are a little too rowdy for polite company."

He arched an eyebrow as he waited for my answer.

While I managed to stifle and play nice, I was still screaming inside. After I had spent ten minutes in the lobby and calmed down enough to think, I remembered to call Larry. I gave him the address, and then continued to wait for any word about Fawn. The link between us slowly faded as the doctors worked to save her and the baby.

I held it together until Larry showed. He was all over me in rage and fear for Fawn, blaming me for what happened. I knew that it was his fear for Fawn talking, but that's what hurt the most. I kept thinking I should have found an excuse to keep Fawn out of it and just gone with the three of us. Fawn really never really gave me a chance to. She dealt herself in, and that was that. In truth, none of us would have made it out without her being there. I can rationalize that, but my gut still says I was wrong to let her come.

I held it together until Larry showed. He was all over me in rage and fear for Fawn, blaming me for what happened. I knew that it was his fear for Fawn talking, but that's what hurt the most. I kept thinking I should have found an excuse to keep Fawn out of it and just gone with the three of us. Fawn really never really gave me a chance to. She dealt herself in, and that was that. In truth, none of us would have made it out without her being there. I can rationalize that it was the right call, but my gut still says I was wrong.

We sat, paced, and sat some more for five hours, waiting for news. Around three in the morning, a group of exhausted looking men and women emerged from the surgery. Both Larry and I were up and moving as soon as we spotted them. One doctor spotted our approach, and walked to us. He was only a few centimeters taller than me. He was swarthy skinned, with dark chocolate eyes, and sharp features and a large, hooked nose that reminded me of a hawk. His tightly curled salt and pepper hair looked like he'd stuck his finger in an electric socket.

He looked at both of us, then held his hand out to Larry. Larry shook it mechanically, staring at the doctor, hope and despair fighting for dominance in his bloodshot eyes. The doctor tugged his hand out of Larry's tight grip, then offered his hand to me.

"I'm Doctor Harrim. Come with me, and we'll talk about what's happened. If you'll follow me."

We walked with Dr. Harrim to a small room. There was a moderately sized circular table, with six chairs surrounding it. The doctor invited us to sit down. Both Larry and I were tense as hell as we each pulled a chair out to sit on. We were both frightened that Fawn hadn't made it, and that this was where we were going to be told.

Dr. Harrim cleared his throat, then looked at the two of us for a moment before beginning.

"First off, let me say that Mrs. Potter is out of danger, and her and the fetus are both healthy, and resting. She will be able to go home in three to four days if she remains stable." He held up his hand before we had a chance to react. "Let me finish. This isn't the end of things. It took time, as I'm sure you realized, to stabilize her. There were, to use an old saw, complications."

He lowered his hand and Larry stared at the doctor. His hands were clenched so tightly that his hands were white.

"What kind of complications?"

Dr. Harrim looked down for a moment as he considered what to say. He looked up at Larry.

"She has *preeclampsia*. This is a condition that has a sudden spike in blood pressure and water retention. It can be fatal to both the mother and the child. It is an uncommon condition, but one that needs close monitoring." He stopped again, looking down at his hands once more. He didn't look up right away as he spoke. "I have never seen the symptoms this early in a pregnancy, nor with such ..." he paused, looking for a diplomatic term, "intense symptoms. She is going to require constant monitoring at home, and bed rest if her symptoms return."

He looked at Larry. "You will need to be her full-time nurse. This will be very stressful for you. If you can hire someone to help, I would recommend that you do so." He raised his hand once more, stopping Larry from speaking. "I want to warn you also, that the earlier preeclampsia appears, the more difficult, and life-threatening, the delivery will be. I know this is not something you want to hear, but I want you to know exactly what your situation is, without any sugar-coating." Dr. Harrim continued, "Magick can mitigate some of the troubles, but it isn't a cure-all. The disease is very sensitive to Magick, and could cause the condition to worsen dramatically. You need to exercise caution, especially around Magick."

Larry stared hard at the doctor, his hands still clenched tight. He closed his eyes for a moment, then opened them.

"Give me the list of what I need to do, and I'll make sure that it's done." His voice had a determined tone, which made me feel warm, and hopeful. I knew that Larry would do everything, and more, to make sure Fawn would be all right. I would help too. This is the kind of thing families do for each other.

I camped out in the Hospital for two days, sitting with Fawn during visiting hours, not daring to touch her. My biggest fear was that Fawn would go critical if I accidentally fed her power. I couldn't lose her. It was selfish, yeah. I admit it was totally selfish on my part. I wanted her to live so I wouldn't be alone. I wanted the baby to live because I wanted Larry not to be mad at me for endangering them. I wanted to be an aunt. We didn't have relatives that we knew of. Just me and Fawn.

This time, it wasn't me recovering in the hospital from wounds. I wish it was me. I don't know how Fawn did it when I was in the coma after PEI. It tore me apart inside to watch her lie unconscious after all the emergency treatment.

# 35

NINE MONTHS LATER, it happened, just like Dr. Harrim had explained it. Fawn went into labor, and had a heart attack as the contractions started. One emergency Caesarean section later, Fawn had a baby daughter. One electroshock after the delivery, Larry had Fawn back.

It was a rough time before the birth. I quit taking jobs so I could help Larry and Fawn, helping clean house, and do those things the doctors recommended Fawn stay away from.

As for the aftermath at the compound, JC said the vegetation died the day after Fawn and I pushed all that magick into the ground. Animals fled the area and nothing comes close to the electrified fence that's been put around the outside of the place.

To borrow a famous American baseball player's quote, "It's *deja vu* all over again." The ground looks like the lake behind our parent's old cabin before we broke the glass bottle. Everything is twisted, warped, and dead.

Ginny, on Fawn's advice, declared independence from her family. The whole sordid affair dominated the news for weeks afterwards. Lurid tales of physical and mental abuse. Neglect. The family disappeared from the social events calendar. They still have ownership of the company, but Ginny's father, Mr. Andrew Cameron, has no control on any of the boards. The stock tanked, and I'm certain a large amount was snapped up by Mary Holdwell.

Almost as lurid was the arrest and trial of Mrs. Villers. Records and banks were raided by the RCMP, who acted on evidence supplied by Ginny Cameron. Haven School was shut down for an extensive faculty change. Mrs. Gross stayed on as headmistress when it was proven that she was an unwitting and unwilling participant in Mrs. Villers' schemes.

Dean went back to his private detective business after a few days in the hospital. He'd suffered frostbite in his feet from being staked out in the snow. Fortunately, none of the injuries required amputation, and he's doing well. He and JC have started working together, much like I and Zhirk did. I would like to find a partner I could trust like that again. Sinera is good, both as a secretary, and as an investigator. She's not Zhirk. And I can't seem to warm up to her, meaning maybe I have a few unresolved 'Elf' issues still.

I moved into my office on a permanent basis. I put all my stuff in storage and am selling my house to pay bills. I'm back at work again, and taking jobs.

Larry and Fawn managed to patch up the fight between them, but things changed. They're still in love, and love their daughter, but the strain left them both unsure of how to handle that big rift they made when Fawn chose to go on the raid. Me, I still carry a load of guilt about it. It's the elephant in the room that no one can figure out how to talk about.

Fawn, if the same situation was presented, would do it all over again without even thinking about it. She sees it as her responsibility. It makes her a good cop. Larry, I think, would probably move heaven and earth to join her — or keep her from going. He's gotten the full baseball bat in the face experience of what it means to be married to a cop. I'm hoping they can work it out.

Fawn convinced me to go to a psychiatrist to get some help with the stress of all that's happened. I don't know if it's working. I still have nightmares five nights out of seven.

Larry still won't speak to me, and I understand why. If our positions were reversed, and he'd endangered Fawn like that, I'd have, well, it'd be a lot worse than just not speaking to him. Fawn has talked to him about it being her choice, but I think that's the real trouble. Fawn saw it as her duty; Larry saw it as nearly killing his family. They're happy, and do care for each other, but still, trauma like that changes people.

I'm just happy they haven't stopped me from dropping by to see Zhira. She's four–months–old now, and just started crawling around, Her curiosity is like mine, and she's poking into anything she can.

Life is okay. It could be better — and it sure could be worse. This, right now, is good enough.

# ABOUT THE AUTHOR

J Dark is a latecomer to the writing profession, but enjoying every moment that life will allow. "The best thing to me is writing a story that someone enjoys. If I've made something fun and entertaining for people, it's a win-win."

J Dark lives with a house full of dreams, three cats, and various friends who occasionally drop by and stay for a while. J Dark lives in Kansas, where the winds blow all the time, and, if you blink your eyes, the weather changes.

You can find out more about the works and world of J Dark at *The Pandemonium* (thepandemonium.net).

# YOU MIGHT ALSO ENJOY

## GRIMAULKIN
by L. A. Jacob

*Treading the straight and narrow is not natural to one who summons demons.*

## WAR MAGE
by Jake Logan & L. A. Jacob

*In war, here be dragons.*

## BUILDING BABY BROTHER
by Steven Radecki

*It seemed like a good idea at the time …*

Available from Paper Angel Press in
hardcover, trade paperback, digital, and audio editions.
paperangelpress.com

www.ingramcontent.com/pod-product-compliance
Lightning Source LLC
Chambersburg PA
CBHW050725180626
46814CB00002B/607